Returning Souls

Ernestine B. Colombo

Returning Souls

Cover and Logo drawings by Michael R. Pasciolla

Cover Concept by Debbie O'Byrne of JetLaunch.net, and Ernestine B. Colombo

Front and Back Cover, Spine, and inside Title / Author page Design: © Debbie@JetLaunch.net

LLC Logo Digitized: @fiverr.com

Back Page Author Photograph: Lisa Sorenson

Written by Ernestine B. Colombo

Follow me on Twitter: Ernestine B. Colombo@ErnieColombo

Visit me on Facebook: Ernestine B. Colombo@ErnieAuthor

Visit my Website at www.ernestinecolomboauthor.com and my Book Launch site www.EBCWriter.com

Printed in the United States of America

First Printing: January 2018

Published by: Sojourn Publishing, LLC

Published for: Wind Horse Wordcraft LLC

ISBN: 978-1-62747-255-5
eISBN: 978-1-62747-215-9

WIND HORSE WORDCRAFT LLC

PRAISE FOR *RETURNING SOULS*

This is one of the most inventive manuscripts I have ever edited. Moreover, it is beautifully written, with strong verbs and wonderfully creative descriptions. The characters are strong – even the minor characters, such as The Old One. The inner dialogue of the two main characters is revealing, and shows real emotional growth of both of them throughout this book.

I especially like the idea of a book that explores what I call 'pre-incarnation'. Ernestine expertly switches from Evie to Astara, back to Evie, back to Astara, and finally, back to Evie – without losing the readers.

I think what I liked most about this manuscript is that it calls on the reader to truly think about the possibility – no, likelihood – that reincarnation (and perhaps 'pre-incarnation') actually exist.

This is a fascinating story, beautifully told. It has 'best-seller' written all over it.

— Bill Worth, Editor, and Author of the novels *House of the Sun: A Metaphysical Novel of Maui, The Hidden Life of Jesus Christ: A Memoir,* and the soon-to-be published non-fiction book exploring his 28 –year journey with multiple sclerosis: *Outwitting Multiple Sclerosis: How Forgiveness Helped Me Heal My Brain By Changing My Mind*

I was suddenly propelled through time and emotions from the first paragraph right through to the last page. *Returning Souls* is perfectly woven from the tangle of personal connections through one life into another, and of lessons learned and others postponed. I was immersed in the delicious descriptions of a new world full of intense yet unfamiliar sights, sounds, and tastes. I was emotionally bound to the complexities of relationships as they balanced through time. Fictional or true to life...it is a page turner to the last sentence.

— Sharon CassanoLochman, Author of the novels *Stranded on Thin Ice*, *Man With The Sand Dollar Face*, and soon-to-be published *Spiritual Verse Today Volumes I, II and III*

Courage, wisdom and love for life can be discovered in unimagined places. Join Ernestine Colombo on a multidimensional adventure as she magically weaves a Mesolithic past life and growing up a woman of the 1960s into a near-death experience.

— Georgina Kemm, Author of soon-to-be published *The Shaman's Lover* Trilogy

Ernestine Colombo delivers a passionate coming-of-age story juxtaposed with the harsh realities of adulthood. Honest and raw – this novel is deeply moving and an absolute pleasure to read.

— J.R. Angelella, Author of *Zombie: A Novel*

CHAPTER ONE

I'm in the kitchen when I fall, slumping down to the floor like a sheaf of blank paper. Quiet and clean, very fast. No warning. I think back to a second ago when my body moved around the room absently, making coffee and foaming milk for a latte, starting to feel my feet on the ground, hands reaching for the hard surface of the coffee mug. While my body moved my mind left and wandered out in search of Liliana, tomorrow's visit with Lara and Ashley, what to cook for dinner.

Liliana. She's starting to slow down now. We recently finished another bout of physical therapy sessions to keep her legs and back strong. What else can I do for her? We should go shopping on Monday, that's always fun for her. I need to keep her interested. Do things together.

I'm afraid, just a little afraid.

She's starting to show her age.

Right this minute I have something new to consider. I'm splayed out, my eyes staring at half a footprint that needs to be wiped up, smelling the mineral coolness of the tiles that press up against my cheek, my side, my legs. My mind is no longer wandering. I'm paying close attention.

What happened? What the hell just happened? I review the last ten seconds. Think quick, it's fading. Before the fall, I felt a tap on the – was it the left – temple? Yes. I saw a flash – swift like sparrows swooping into the azaleas, almost not visible, the *impression* of a flash. And a prickly electric connection I think, like holding the wrong wires together. I am already forgetting the moment of impact.

Come back to the kitchen. Think!

My eyes are open.

Blink your eyes!

The eyes don't blink.

I check the other body parts. Legs not moving, no pain, not broken. Lying on my side, weight on my right shoulder and hip, back curved slightly forward, not uncomfortable yet, nothing hurts, probably not broken, but not moving. Mouth open, can't swallow, tongue between teeth, everything starting to dry out. Teeth not hurting, probably not broken. Heart – strange rhythm and loud, it's so loud, someone else must be able to hear it.

Liquid still beats through me, like surf.

Is my face wet? No, not bleeding.

Fingers don't move. Legs don't move. I'll call Paul. Dry throat, everything dry, tongue doesn't move, no sound comes out.

Slap the tiles, make some noise. My arm belongs to another body. Not mine anymore.

A swift clicking of claws on tile. Olive finds me. My cat, the one I hand-raised from a pathetic runt to silver gray sleekness, skitters to my side. Is this a new game, he wants to know? He knows everything the instant it happens, he can hear insects walk in the dark, he anticipates my thoughts. He hesitates for a split second, and – this is not a game. He shoves his wet lavender nose onto my face. Sniffs deeply. Rubs the length of his body against my cheek. Smooth fur, some of it in my mouth now. I can still feel. I am encouraged.

Olive meows inquiringly, sharp yellow eyes peering into my unblinking hazel ones, his expression serious. I smell fish breath. He meows louder, paces back and forth quickly, rubs his teeth against my cheek.

I try to say, *No Olive, you're getting hair in my mouth.*

Throat still not working. The meow escalates to a yowl.

He disappears.

The yowl recedes; he has left me alone here. Getting chilly now. Paul is probably doing his morning reading. I predict he will ignore Olive. I listen. Yes. In a moment Olive is back, chirps, nips my cheek.

I'm sorry Olive, I can't move. Don't bite Mommy. It hurts – doesn't it? It used to.

Olive runs away again with another yowl. Do I hear a muffled sound of Paul asking him what he wants? He probably thinks Olive is hungry. Italians think food fixes everything. This will be a rude awakening for someone.

Olive leaps back into the kitchen ahead of Paul, all legs and lithe grace. The volume of Paul's voice gets louder as he talks to Olive. He's coming in, so now what? I begin to feel disinterested in what is happening. Everything is taking too long.

Anyway, I can move again on my own.

Move – what? My eyelids? No. My arm? No.

But not worried at all. Light. I'm light. I sense glimmers enter the room. What are they? My hearing picks up an interrupted sound of meow, the prominent click of grey claws back and forth, and the approach of Paul's voice. Too much noise, too cold down here. Glimmers like shapes with faces I know, beautiful like morning on water, intriguing like a scent of dark seaweeds twining with sand and broken clams. The glimmers are replaced incrementally with a sound of surf pulling shells and pebbles back and forth, in and out, breathing, lulling me to calmness. I dwell on the glimmers of a memory, a place, a time when I was happy, or of a time before I can remember.

I'm losing track.

Can I get up now please? It seems I have only to think it and I drift up and away.

First a foot or two, now three, now four, five, six.

I can see better from up here.

A sudden thought – Liliana! I can't leave her alone here. No! Not now! Who will take care of her, make sure she's okay? Yes, I have a Will, but who will care about *her*, who will understand her? I can't think about this. I can't focus. I don't have a choice.

Olive is back again, his eyes insistent as he looks at my still body. He implores me, *Mommy, stay.*

I think he sees me lift, since his eyes remain focused on mine as I float slowly upward. Should I tell him it's okay? It seems less and less important with each moment. I rise without sound, without effort, without movement. I watch as Paul finally enters the room. His chest moves like it has been jolted by one of those machines that restart the heart. His mouth opens dark and red in a round shape and his hands flap down toward my body. I can't hear him or Olive's meows or anything clearly except for the surf sound that cleanses without moisture, refreshes like a silken touch or ancient rhythm. Foamy surf turns to pale green water that forms a window through which I watch the activities below.

Now Paul shakes the unmoving body by the shoulders. His lips form words I can't hear. They look like, *Honey? Talk to me! What happened? Can you hear me?*

Quickly he drops to one knee, hands flat on the floor, elbows bent, and peers into my face. I'm curious. My vision lasers down to his mouth. He's talking to the body.

"Evie, Honey, my God, wake up!"

His brown eyes are wide and glisten with wetness, his chest rises and falls quickly, I hear his heart pound loudly and though I don't hear his words very well anymore, I hear the rush of his dark blood flowing, adamant in his hands and his legs and his heart, pushing him into action.

I feel deeply sad that I can't tell him anything. I'm sorry. So sorry. I'm in here. I can't get out right now. Paul, I don't want you to worry. I'll be all right.

He puts his ear to my chest – smooth black hair with some silver coming in, gold earring, scruff of day-old beard, tears falling in my mouth – and jumps up. He runs to another room, comes back quickly dialing a number into his phone, and in a few seconds he is talking excitedly, gesturing at the phone and the room in a controlled frenzy. Olive is back, yowling. The two other cats, Moose and Chloe, have come into the room now. Moose takes up watch, leaning his twenty-one pounds of Maine Coon cat possessively into the body, with one large white paw extended onto an unmoving hand. Chloe stands in the doorway, pale eyes like saucers, tail puffed out in fear and shock. They are all visible, but a transparent surf has formed a gauze over the scene and I'm having trouble seeing colors.

Why surf? Why am I not wet?

The seconds fall like old sepia snapshots flipping one after the other to make a moving picture. I'm high above the apartment building, but still able to see all the movement in the kitchen through the surfy gauze. As far as I can tell the body hasn't moved on its own. I hear sirens. Paul runs out the apartment door, down the walkway and into the street, arms waving over his head, his dark hair loose around his face.

"Over here!" he shouts and waves his arms.

The ambulance stops. Flashing lights cast red figures against the building facade. Ambulance doors fly open and stretcher apparatus bounces out onto the sidewalk and is pulled and shoved loudly into the apartment, the wheels spinning round and round as they hit the pavement, the door jamb, the oak parquet, and finally stop in the kitchen. I lower in for a better look. A man and woman in matching outfits check the body. The woman touches the neck with two fingers. They look at each other and together without speaking they lift the body onto the stretcher and swiftly wheel it out into the living room, into the foyer, and out the door. The stretcher bounces crazily down the walk as the figures run alongside, pushing it toward open ambulance doors. The runners have found time to attach tubes into the nose and a canister of some kind lays beside the body on the stretcher. I don't wait to hear where they are taking the body. Instead, I zoom back into the apartment. The cats have scattered except for Moose, who has followed the stretcher to the entrance door, craning his head to see where they are taking his Mom. Paul pushes him back into the foyer with an open palm before slamming the door, locking it and running after the stretcher and into his car.

He yells after the figures as they start up the motor of the ambulance.

"What hospital are we going to?"

A few neighbors have opened their doors and study the scene so they can exchange information later about who is sick and the sequence of events. Car and ambulance doors slam and all the vehicles leave quickly in a stink of exhaust and dissipating smoke. I can hear the sirens recede from loud to dim, and see tail lights fade. My attention drifts back to the apartment.

Where's Olive?

I drift around easily. The surf sound is more in the background now, still soothing. The surf gauze parts as I drop lightly down into the living room.

I see the yellow eyes first. Olive has been hiding behind the bookcase, but now that everyone is gone he creeps slowly into the room, every hair standing out from his body. He crouches, listens, looks, and sniffs the tracks left by stretcher wheels on the oak parquet. He creeps over to where the body was, starts to yowl, and looks upward.

I see deep into yellow eyes, my Olive's eyes, and they seem to get bigger while the apartment gets smaller. Olive's upturned face and open pink mouth become even smaller as I rise through the gauze until his face and body are miniscule. But the yellow eyes get bigger, and softer, and wider, and sadder, until the whole Earth and sky are pale, glowing gold and the eyes are gone.

❦

Drifting. Above the white clouds, above the wind.

I put out my arms and legs and arch my neck backward. My hair moves around my face like I'm under water. My skin feels distended. I could break open and bleed into the surroundings, disperse atom by atom into the clouds, the air, but I decide to stay intact and rest timelessly, watching clouds change their shape and color in silence.

I am light, as if years of sediment have lifted into the atmosphere and drifted away from me. Air wafts through me, clearing my tissues of the detritus of life. I may not be breathing but it is of no concern. There is no sound except for the constant flow of air snapping and billowing me like a new flag in the wind. In the background is a distant sound of ocean surf pounding everything into a pleasant nothing.

Above and around me the mega trillions of stars are rimmed in light. Stars spread out in a swirling cape behind, over and beyond my vision, yet each individual star is lit to show itself like a jewel. A vast curve of pale pink horizon arches into dusk, doming upward into gradual gold, green, teal, Gulf Stream indigo, finally darkest purple strewn with the stars.

If I look down, edges of iridescent green leaves reach up like soothing hands. They do not beckon but are simply joyous, triumphant, imperceptibly winding and spreading, lush with sap.

What is this place?

Light fills all objects and when they can hold no more a molten purity lances out from their many pores and imbues everything else. I look at my hands outspread in front of my face; they glow glacial blue and throb with inner life.

Is this what it feels like to truly be alive?

Or am I dead?

Dead.

I wasn't ready for it, wasn't expecting it. I wasn't ill. After sixty-odd years on Earth I was finally getting used to being there. I was eating clean and going green. Granted I was a slow learner. Many mistakes led me to this insipid culmination, with so much time ahead of me. I was a traveler with no itinerary, no plan or direction. For so many decades I looked frantically toward other people to be my anchor, my reason.

Do I get a chance now to review the journey and correct my course? Which mistake should I correct? There were so many. Who can I talk to about do-overs? Does any of that matter now?

My questions boom inside my head but there is still no sound except the wind and surf.

The time to ask for help is past.

As if on cue a cavalcade of vignettes parade by like an old fashioned newsreel: a garden, the scent of freshly dug earth, soil under my nails; faces around a coffee table, television on and nobody watching; dusty smell of wires running under industrial tiles, fluorescent hum, rows of computer screens; wrinkled olive-skinned faces flickering by firelight; a band of humans loping easily through dim forest; women laughing together by the sea, naked under the slanting morning sun; dazzle of sunlit water, a silvery fish flexing on a spear.

When I think I recognize an image it's forgotten and I'm trying to recognize the next one.

I gain some heft and drift away from the pink horizon and jewel rimmed stars, toward the treetops, between leaves, past deeply textured tree trunks, like a dead leaf twisting toward brown decomposition. I come to rest on a resinous bed of pine needles, neon green moss, new ferns twirling open in fibonacci perfection, acorn tops, and an occasional live seed cracking open to reveal two piercingly green fleshy leaves.

I think I'll rest here and wait to see what finds me. Silly. It's not as if I have a choice. It is quiet except for moist rivulets of dew that collect into a thin flow dripping in front of my nose. I hear the eternal sounds of vegetation settling, leaf melding with branch, branch bending against stone. Maybe I don't want to move.

Who am I kidding? Of course I want to move! I want to do everything I used to do. And now I'm stuck here. And exactly where is here? One thing's for sure, I can't do this for eternity. Move an arm, a leg, anything.

Wake up!

Wake up and stand on your own two feet!

You are a grown woman of the tribe now.

You saw your visions and you know who you are.

Get up! Do not be afraid.

Wait a minute. Whose voice is that?

Who is talking in my head?

Will somebody please tell me what's going on?

CHAPTER TWO

I should stop trying to force myself to move. I've had a bad shock. Dying is probably in the category of a bad shock. Don't panic. Go with the flow. I'm a rotting leaf left to contemplate its journey as it disintegrates into soil. I have time to deeply concentrate on the trajectory of my life, on the life of a person that was me. Me? Which me? I'm Evie of course.

If I want to get up I need to forget about Evie and be myself.

Whose voice is in my head? My voice, of course! It sounds like my voice. Open my eyes and see where I am. The smells are familiar, rich and comforting.

Come on. What are you afraid of?

And now. My eyes are open.

Green leaves, sticks and rocks. I'm lying on my side as though I fell asleep here. Branches and shrubby leaves push at my back. Lifting my head to look ahead, I see massive tree trunks. The trilling of an unseen thrush echoes in a song that is hauntingly beautiful, familiar, but slightly different than I remember, a new morph of the Hermit or possibly the Song Thrush. I'm rusty on my thrushes. I lie with cheek to floor again as I did in my kitchen back home, but this floor is earth instead of tile. Instead of footprints left for me to clean up there are no prints, just moss and leaves. There is a feeling of newness here.

Resting in the potpourri of vegetation turning to earth, listening to bird song and a snuffling of some animal a way off, I feel exposed.

Should I not move from here?

Or am I lying here out of design?

Gather my thoughts. I feel whole and strong with nothing broken. I lifted my head up. I can move! But an overriding thought comes to me – *move quietly!* I am probably safe now. Listen. Do not even breathe. Listen for any familiar sound before I move. Make sure I am alone.

I lie without moving and listen intently, breathing soundlessly, taking in every smell of the forest. Is it familiar? Am I alone? It is important that I am alone while I get my bearings. One wrong move and I could fall into the wrong hands, and then what will become of me?

Fall into the wrong hands! What hands are those? These are strange thoughts.

The important thing right now is that no one is here, so for the moment I am safe. I can get up now.

Slowly I move my arms and legs and in a smooth soundless movement, roll onto hands and knees. The ease with which I have gotten into this position is astounding. My stomach aches – hunger. I stiffen to control my head, waiting for the familiar arthritic neck pain that will shoot like a knife up into my skull any second now. I wait for it, and wait some more, but the pain does not come. I feel good. Very, very good. Better than I remember feeling for a long time, maybe ever.

I am on my hands and knees, and then jump my feet together behind my hands and stand quickly, looking right and left and listening to every sound of the forest, moving like an accomplished Yogini or ballet dancer, strong and warm. Then I notice them – my hands and my feet look different. Young. They decidedly do not look like *my* hands and feet. At least, my hands and feet have not looked this young in ages.

And yet this is me, the hands and feet are my own, and these are my thoughts. I hold my arms out in front of me and swivel them around to get a good look and feel. Without arthritis pain I can move my head around to examine myself.

My arms are long, wiry and quite tan. I look down at well-muscled legs, scarred on the knees and shins especially, some scars old and some rather recent. I scratch my head, and pull a long braid of hair forward in an unconscious movement that calms me down as I play with the ends. The hair is dark, not quite black, very long and twisted in a single plait that is starting to come loose. Suddenly I drop the braid like it's red hot.

Since when is my hair dark and three feet long?

I become aware of my outfit, if that is what it is. It is a garment made of light brown hide, deer or goat skin, a sleeveless dress or a shift, very soft but not very warm. No matter – the weather is temperate. I check to see if I am wearing underwear and find something strappy and pliable between my legs, held on with another strap around my waist. It looks as if it is made of very soft thin hide or some kind of soft fiber, and while it seems to be put together by hand it is not at all uncomfortable.

I am standing here in a quiet wood among trees of huge dimension wearing clothing made of hide, and as I listen for human sounds I am relieved to confirm that I am alone.

This is *really* strange.

I have not moved my feet since I stood up. I feel this body take a few steps toward the nearest tree with an unaccustomed animal grace and stealth. Is there moss on one side of the tree trunk and can I see the sky peeking between the high boughs? Yes, but the light is weak down here, and the trees are massive with a shaggy soft bark of beautiful russet brown. The forest smell is clean and not too damp.

I am a long way from my home.

I see that I am quite dirty, but I have no odor and my skin is smooth. The freedom with which I move tells me this body is that of a girl of perhaps eleven or twelve years, lithe but strong, in perfect command of every movement. My senses are fine-tuned to tabulate every detail of my surroundings: scent, sound, wind or lack thereof, intensity of light, kind of trees, plants, mosses, boulders, stumps and other features so I can find my way back again.

But to where?

I am hungry and more important, thirsty. I breathe deeply, trying to smell water on the air. Yes, the scent is unmistakable although I gauge I will need to walk a distance to find it.

Did I just smell water?

I start walking past the tallest tree, picking my way silently through bracken and rocks under foot, watching for large boulders or shrubs that will make good landmarks. I notice I am not wearing shoes. The cool earth feels good underfoot. I say a silent prayer to Gaia and the forest, thanking them for shielding me. As I pick my way through the woods there is a slightly cooler feel to the air, an earthier smell, and a dim rushing sound gets louder. I take longer steps to quicken my pace toward running water while still moving soundlessly, not even brushing against the leaves. Almost there. The sound of water is loud now.

The swiftly running stream is ahead at a slight break in the thickness of trees. I stop, scenting the air once again, look right and left, and drop soundlessly into a crouch. There could be strange people here. Check carefully before taking another step. Though my skin color is a camouflage against the ground, I barely breathe.

Fascinated by my thought process, I don't wonder or worry; I observe this sure-footed young body taking me where it needs to go. I'm two people within one body, shifting in and out of an inner dialog, but I surrender to the young girl more and more with each passing second. I remember being Evie but not Evie, wanting to review my journey. This is my chance. Don't fight it.

Mental shapes of language and memory transform into shapes that are familiar and known, yet at the same time alien and long forgotten: clearings, large boulders marking a left turn, a warm cave rich with the smell of people – men, women, children – my tribe.

In the back of my mind I think, *Have I died and come back as someone else? Who am I? Where am I?*

So many questions, but at least one answer comes in a rush.

My name is Astara.

I am lost, or rather, separated from my people. My focus now is to get back into my tribal territory before the people who live on this side of the forest find me. If they catch me, I will probably never see my family again. If the people from this side do not kill me, they will keep me a captive and I will have to live my life as one of them, be joined to one of their men, cook their food, and follow their rituals. And I do not want to do any of that.

Find water and something to eat. Get back to my tribe's land with speed and silence. My life depends on it.

I have been through a lot. It was quite a ride. I enjoyed drifting, the view from above was incredible, falling into the forest as a dry leaf was a deeply relaxing and primal experience, but this is strange. I need answers.

Here is an answer: I need water.

I meld into the girl who is Astara, rising slowly from my defensive crouch and taking a silent step toward the cold brook that flows a few feet in front of me. With muscles ready to explode with speed, at the same time I stoop down again to drink the clear cool water, delicately flipping it into my mouth with the fingers of my left hand. So I am left-handed. I always thought I should have been a lefty, but my mother always discouraged me.

"We don't have any left-handed people in our family Evelyn."

Evelyn. Evie. That is also me. I am Astara and I am Evie.

Confusing. Let it go.

I review how I got to this part of the forest and where I want to go after drinking water and finding food. I had been running for my life as I recall, but why?

The answer flashes into my brain in the most natural way. Yesterday I completed my Girl's Coming of Age Rite, in which a group of girls from the tribe are given something magical to drink by the Grandmothers, and we go on a vision quest. This is our people's mystical rite of passage into our future lives as women of the Golden Fish tribe. Our vision is supposed to show what our role will be within the tribe for the rest of our life.

I might have seen myself as one of the women who gather herbs and roots for healing. Or as one of the group of women who process animal skins into clothing, water bags and foot coverings. If my vision included beadwork or designs it would be an important foretelling, because this would show that I was to be one of the elite group of women who create sacred garb for The Old One, and the ceremonial clothing worn by a man and woman when they are joined. The beadwork on the men's garments tells the story of past deeds of valor in the hunt or during conflicts with the Forest tribes. The beadwork on the woman's joining garment usually shows the visions the woman saw during the rite of passage ceremony. Woman rarely perform deeds of valor but if they have done anything out of the ordinary, that action would be sewn into the beadwork of their joining garment.

I laugh when I think of my joining garment. I have done things that women of our tribe never do. I saved Tonna's baby Lun from rolling into the hot coals of the communal hearth by leaping across the fire and catching the child in my arms, and I have the scars to prove it. I made traps of willow and reed and caught small birds and rabbits in them so that Mother and I would not starve during the time of no animals. I still weave fish traps that look like baskets, and use long lines twisted from reeds and vines to catch fish in the surf, attaching sharp hooks made from bone and sticking bits of meat on for bait. Father used to hunt for us, but he was lost on the big hunt three seasons past when the men went out farther than usual for large game. Now it is just Mother and me. I have done a lot for a girl. My joining garment will be a challenge for any of the women to make.

But now I know I will never have such a garment.

I did not see anything a girl is supposed to see. I could not tell this to the Grandmothers or the old hunter Shawlee who watched over us during our quest. I knew I had to run away before I was brought back to the tribe to complete the ritual that would make me a Golden Fish tribe woman.

I am not a normal woman. My vision quest brings the confusing pieces of my life into focus and everything makes sense to me. I may look like a woman on the outside – a girl, for now – but in my vision I had a powerful body that belonged sometimes to a dire wolf and other times to a charging stag. I was not male or female or animal, but all three rolled into one.

When we were children we sat every evening in Spirit Circle with The Old One to learn our heritage. The Old One stood in the center of a circle of children, wearing his dirty leather cloak and headdress, twisting and swinging his tall body upward and then down to the ground to act out stories of things we would never see. Things only he could see. One story told about the Three Face, who was at once man, woman, and animal. Even as a little child I giggled at his antics. I knew the stories were not real.

I was wrong.

By now the Grandmothers, Shawlee and the girls must be back with the tribe. The custom is to wait two days and nights for a missing member to return. If I am not back by then, there might be a tribal meeting to decide whether to search for me.

I do not want the tribe to search for me, or worse, to decide I am not worth searching for.

I want to tell Mother what I saw on my quest. I hope she will believe me.

Someone has to believe me. The thought of joining with one of the boys and living through the regular role of a woman in the tribe makes me feel sick to my stomach.

I am a Three Face. My life will be a Spiritual journey. I saw myself alone in a cave with paintings on the ceiling and walls. I fished for food and gathered herbs for rituals. I traveled far away to meet other tribes and learn their customs. There were others like me and together we showed all the tribes new ways of life. A Three Face is a leader, not a follower.

The strap between my legs is getting damp. I need more moss – but which kind? Mother will know.

What is the point of having a vision if nobody will let you follow it? I wonder if The Old One will recognize and accept me.

Stop thinking so much! I need to find food. Some fruit or a root. My eyes sweep the ground. Here, by the stream, a thick green vine is growing toward a patch of sun. I grasp the base firmly at ground level and give it a gentle twist. A pale tuber rips up easily. I swish it clean in the cold stream, and begin to munch on its crisp white flesh.

I turn soundlessly and begin running back toward the rocky cliffs and the Great Water.

CHAPTER THREE

It is taking too long to find my way back to the spot where I woke up. I thought I was being clever to choose a path over hardscrabble. I thought no one would be able to track me, and I was right.

I cannot track myself.

Too near the border of Forest tribe territory! I turn in a circle. Is *anything* familiar?

That tree. The pattern of the moss growing on the trunk has the shape of a chipmunk. I noticed it when I woke up.

Get your bearings. Get away from this part of the forest.

Make no sound.

Move toward the Great Water.

I move more quickly now that I know where I am going. When I reach the cave where the Girls' Rite was, no trace of us remains. No food parcels, no footprints in the cave, no ashes or smell of fires. The Grandmothers and Shawlee were thorough in removing all trace of our time here.

I track my way back toward the caves where my tribe lives. We are the Golden Fish tribe, named for the small fishes that make up the bulk of our food source. The skin of these fish is as much silver as gold, with as much red and blue. The beauty and huge numbers of these fish is legendary. As a food source, they sustain our people. The Great Water gives us our life.

Picking my way across boulder-strewn ground I imagine what the tribe is doing and where Mother will be. By now the Grandmothers and the old hunter Shawlee have led the rest of the girls back to the tribal compound. There were only eight girls in the rite. Our tribe is neither big nor small, with an average number of girls who will perpetuate our tribe into the coming generations. No one is wondering why I did not return with the rest of the girls. I have disappeared before.

When I finally return and find Mother, then what?

Over the years I have been a source of joy and sustenance to her, and also of embarrassment. Bold deeds bring acclaim, but anyone who is different is suspect. My mother has invented many stories to explain away my differences.

The most noticeable difference is that I never want to play with the other girls or learn girl activities, which involve sitting still and sewing or cutting up roots for food. I enjoy kicking a thick hide ball and running with the boys, but more often I prefer to be alone in the forest listening to birds and taming ground squirrels and mice. My best friend is Varno, the Leader's youngest son. He and I have spent many afternoons climbing fig trees to find the best fruit, or scaling the sea cliffs, holding on to sharp crags with our fingers and toes. It is not the usual way that young girls and boys interact, but my mother and the Leader accept the friendship without question.

When I saved Tonna's baby Lun from the fire it was a heroic deed, but not the deed of a young girl. The emotions of the tribe were mixed. There was joy that Lun was safe and unharmed, and unease that a young girl had been the one to see him falling and to dive without thinking over the hot coals of the fire, literally snatching the child in mid-air before even an ember touched his tender skin. Everyone had looked at Mother after they had absorbed both the joy and uniqueness of the incident. What was she doing different, or wrong, that made her daughter so unlike the other girls?

Mother herself noticed my differences from the time I was young, but I am her daughter. We are a team. Mother knows me better than anyone else on Gaia. She probably already knows I am a Three Face.

The terrain is familiar. Thank Gaia! I am back in my tribe's territory. We are fifty people, one of the largest tribes on the coastline. Our leader, Savvo, is an impressive man of wisdom, physical strength, a warrior's spirit, and a hunter's knowledge of place and prey. He has always been kind to Mother and me.

It is coming onto dusk. When it is dark I will creep through the tribal circle and slip into our tent. Mother will be there waiting for me. Or she will be with Savvo, the elders and The Old One, worried and deciding what to do about my disappearance. If she is not in the tent I will wait in the shadows until I see her return, and then I will come home and explain everything.

I hear conversation as I prowl the edges of the tribal compound, mostly about the newly initiated girls who shared the Girl's Coming of Age vision quest. Raynata's voice is filled with excitement as she tells everyone she saw herself joined with

Savvo's eldest son, Petano. Claps and shouts burst out at her family's fire. Raynata is the most beautiful of the tribe's girls, with long blue-black hair and pale eyes like the green ripples moving under the Great Water. Everyone will be happy to see her mated with Petano. He is physically strong and does not rush to judgment, good qualities for a future leader of our tribe. Their children are sure to be beautiful.

I hear excitement at other fires. Tunnara saw herself mated with my best friend, Varno. Oh no! Tunnara is the worst possible match for him. I try to like everyone in the tribe, but she is mean and makes up bad stories about people. Varno deserves someone kind and smart. Tunnara will be a stupid, selfish mate and will raise annoying children. She has a big nose and thick hair like a pelt that does not stop at her head, but extends to her cheeks and upper lip. I do not believe Tunnara's vision; Varno would never choose her!

I listen at fire after fire. Nobody is talking about my disappearance. Maybe nobody thinks it is strange.

I walk past our tent and see Mother's silhouette through the yellowed skin. There are other silhouettes too. I creep closer to listen.

"She has been gone before. I know she will be back very soon. Give her some time to return before we send out a search party." Mother's voice, with a slight quiver.

"That child of yours is always starting trouble. Why must she always be different from the other girls? She is unpredictable. We do not need a girl who will not do her part within the tribe."

It is The Old One. His voice is deep and the words come out in a gravelly slur. He has never liked me, probably because I laughed at his stories when we children sat with him in Learning Circle. He, or She, or It, hated that.

Nobody knows whether The Old One is man or woman. He wears a hide robe and a molded leather headdress with a row of leather-strung cowrie shells that fall in a straight line down over the eyes. Nobody even knows if he has eyes. But The Old One sees everything.

Another voice – Savvo.

"Old One, I hear your words and I do not see a problem. Astara is a good girl. She is not unpredictable, she simply does not act like the other girls. She is bold, more like a boy, but I do not find that to be a problem. She watches over the other children, especially the young ones who can so easily get hurt. Let us not forget about how she saved Lun from the fire."

The Old One groans like that was not important.

"Let me finish," continues Savvo. "She knows more about the forest and the Great Water than any other girl or woman in the tribe. Do not forget, she has provided for herself and Orana every day since Ruano was lost in the winter hunt. It is good that she is not afraid to do many things the other girls cannot do. Because of her, she and Orana have not been a burden. Astara is a valuable member of our tribe."

Good. I always thought Savvo liked me, but now I know for certain. This is information that could save my life if The Old One turns on me. That old bag of bones is not even human, he is an *it*. And I do not trust it at all.

Mother's voice again. "Please, give her one more night. I have a strong feeling my girl will return tonight. We will not need to waste the efforts of the men on her account, I promise you both!" Pleading with them. Why?

What if The Old One will not acknowledge my vision?

No time to worry about that now. He and Savvo are coming out of our tent. I scuttle back against the shrubs and trees and hold my breath. Savvo tunes his senses to the other tribal fires as he moves with a steady step toward the center of the compound. The Old One stops after walking a few paces, and turns to face the exact spot where I am hiding in the dark.

I shut my eyes, lower my head and crouch down to the ground so I will not be seen. I do not breathe or move a muscle.

"Are you coming?" Savvo asks impatiently.

"I sense something lurking," the deep voice drones, "perhaps the girl Astara sneaking in the dark. She is not to be trusted." I curl my hands into fists so my light-colored fingernails will not give me away.

"If it is Astara we should be glad. She will come home to her mother and all will be well," Savvo says lightly. "Come, let us talk to the rest of the families to see how the other girls fared on their vision quests." His strong profile is turned toward the center of the compound and his posture is poised to move on to new conversations.

The Old One shuffles after Savvo, turning its head back several times. Finally they both leave the area of our tent.

Wait. The Old One may double back when Savvo becomes engaged at another fire.

I wait. Nobody comes back. I can move now.

Crawling on hands and knees to the tent I whisper loudly. "Mother. It is me." I stick my head into the tent with a big smile.

"Come in, Daughter! I have been waiting for you." Mother taps her hand on a soft sitting cushion stuffed with sweet grass and worn hide remnants. "I knew you would come back tonight. Where have you been?"

I crawl in all the way and fall into her arms. Her warm embrace and familiar scent of tanned hides and cooking fires relaxes me. I did not realize how tense I was. Mother always smells like home.

"What happened at the vision quest Astara? Why did you run away?" Her grip on me stiffens. "Did you see something?"

"I saw things that the other girls did not see, so I ran away," I say simply, sitting up.

"You are such a silly girl sometimes," she says, running her fingers through her light brown hair, pushing it back from her brow. "Why do you think the other girls did not see what you saw?"

"They saw mates, and children, and joining, and tanning hides, and cooking."

"That is what all the girls see."

"Not me."

"What are you saying?" She blinks her eyes quickly.

"I lived in a cave. Alone. I ran through the forest like a wolf, without any garments. I do not know if I was man, woman or beast. There is a name for it, a Three Face. The Old One told us the stories."

"Oh," is all Mother can say. She has been squatting in front of me while I describe my vision, but now she rocks back on her heels and sits down with a thump. She stares at me as if I pushed her down with my hand.

"You must believe me. Do you not see why I had to run away?" *Why am I speaking so fast?*

"Yes." Her voice is slow and tired. "I see that you always have to be different, as The Old One says. I see..."

I cut her off excitedly.

"I am not different because I am trying to prove something, or pretending to be different. I *am* different!" I hiss at her. I want to shout and jump and gesture. "You know me. You *must* know I am not like the other girls!" I am still whispering, but getting louder.

"Hush, my child. You are right. I *have* known you are different from the time you were a baby, but I did not want to believe it. Being different makes life harder for everyone. Since your father was killed, I have been afraid of losing you too. What will happen to you if you are not like the other girls of our tribe?" Her chin shakes and she blinks quickly.

I want to cry for my mother, but I do not have time for tears. "I am a Three Face. The Old One used to tell us stories about them and I used to laugh at him, but now I see he was right. I may look like a girl on the outside, but inside I am something different. I cannot go through a joining ceremony with one of these boys. I will kill myself first. Or run away."

My words surprise me. Do I truly mean I will kill myself? The idea of joining makes my stomach crawl.

Mother looks at me, then down into her lap. Her chin trembles and tears drip down her neck now. She wipes at the wetness slowly, breathes in and out deeply. She stops crying and smooths her unruly hair behind her ears again.

"Your father would be so proud of you." She inhales like she is out of breath. "If this is your vision then I believe you must follow it. The quest is taken seriously for all the other girls. Your quest should be taken seriously too." Mother reaches her arms out and I fall against her skin. With her arms around me I can feel myself shaking. She smooths my tangled braid and absently picks out remnants of leaf and stick.

She continues quietly. "The visions you have seen make sense to me. I know the truth of where you come from. The right thing to do now is to approach The Old One with your vision, but I am not sure if it is the safe thing to do."

I cringe against her and look up. Her face is serene and she looks at a spot on the wall of the tent. "Why is telling The Old One not safe?" I have been feeling the same thing but I do not know why.

"Your father loved you very much. You were his pride. None of the other girls in the tribe can do the things you can do. And he accepted you even though you had those eyes."

"Well of course he accepted me! I am his daughter! And what about my eyes?" I have been hearing about my eyes my whole life but since I cannot see them I never paid much attention.

"Shhh, keep your voice low dear. Your father, Ruano, accepted you because he loved you from the moment you were born. But he knew." She trails off and her skin, so warm a few moments ago, raises in bumps as a shiver runs through her.

"He knew what?"

"Ruano was not your *real* father," she says simply. She folds my hands into hers and looks into my eyes.

I do not know what to say. I let the words fall though me. "If Ruano is not my father then who is he?"

"He was a kind man, a brave warrior, and a skilled hunter and provider. He was the tribe's most gifted scout. He was loving toward me and he adored you, his wild and beautiful daughter." She sighs and stops talking.

"You are trying to tell me he is not my father?" I feel a sudden urge to run, and start to get up.

"Another man of the Great Water People is your *real* father," she says, grasping me by my shoulders with strong hands and shoving me back down.

"What other man?" I demand. I have seen men and women together in the shadowy edge of the camp, or heard them laughing and scrabbling around in the shrubs during the spring and autumn celebrations. Did Mother do something like that with another man?

"You must understand, I was an innocent young girl and did not know so many things then as I do now. When you are young you are so full of respect for the Holy rituals of the tribe and the leaders."

I cut her off. "Are you saying you did something with another man of the tribe? When did that happen? Where was Father?"

"I loved Ruano. You know that. We were happy. But I was not always destined to be joined with him." She sighs and goes on. "I was not born to the Golden Fish tribe."

I feel dizzy.

"You came from another tribe? A rival? Not the Dolphin tribe! Were you lost? Or taken?"

She stares over my head and goes on. "I came to our Golden Fish tribe as a young girl. I had to run away from my own people, the Great Cliff tribe. I was cast out, really. I came by myself, but with you in my belly."

"You were with child. And Father found you." My hands are open, palms up, waiting for something. "Why did you have to run away from your own tribe? You ended up having a baby no matter what tribe you were part of."

She takes a deep breath and looks at me. "Dear, have you eaten anything today?"

"A root. But I am not very hungry."

"You do not know how hungry you are. You must eat something."

I do not bother to stop her as she reaches into a basket behind her and retrieves a strip of smoked bonito, oily and sweet and salty all at once. We cure fish and meat with salt that we dry out of the Great Water. It has a subtle flavor and preservative powers. The sea gives us so much.

"Here dear, you have had a long trek all on your own."

I take the strip of fish and absently chew. It is *so* good. Everyone knows Mother makes the best smoked fish. All her food is the best. That may be why I grew strong with straight white teeth. Not everyone has a mother like mine.

"I am ready to listen," I say between mouthfuls of fish.

"I was very young, probably your age or a year older. In my tribe we had a person like our Old One here. A Holy person. And he had acolytes."

"What is an acolyte?" I cannot stop myself from interrupting.

"I am going to tell you, eat your fish and listen. He had students – the acolytes – and there was one in particular whom I had known from the time we were very young."

"His name was – is – Thanillo. He and I were friends like you and Varno. We did everything together from the time we were small children. As he got older he became quiet and wanted to learn secret things. Tribal lore. He was chosen from among the group of young boys coming of age to be an acolyte of the Holy One of my tribe."

Mother had a friend, like Varno and me. It is hard to imagine my life without Varno, but I try. I stare into the fire burning low in the center of our tent and feel myself sink into a hole where Varno should be. Faces melt in the flames, but not Varno's.

A log cracks into the fire. My eyes fly open, then close against the glare.

Drawn toward a soft glob of light, I rise and roost like an invisible bird. My eyes fly over a scene of whole roasted boar set out on a bed of leaves, and antlers of a giant deer lying on the ground at one end of a clearing. Twisting shadows of people dancing move like fingers over the ground. Several young men, the acolytes, beat madly on drums made from animal skins pulled taut and dried to fit over hollow gourds the size of a man's torso.

My eyes flap open. Are there people in our tent?

Mother is here. Relax. Go back.

I exhale in the dark. There she is. A shapely girl with fluffy brown hair catches my attention. Many hands shove cups filled with a liquid at her. She hesitates, sniffs at one of the cups, drinks, stares blankly into the cup for a while, drinks again, and looks up as if someone has called her name.

Her head swings toward the drummers.

She stares blankly for a few more seconds, then walks with halting steps through the throng, stopping in front of the loudest drummer, transfixed by his pumping arms and white teeth glimmering between parted lips. Sweat courses down his chest and legs and flies from his arms as he drums like a blind man with eyes rolled back, swaying as if he will fall.

She is drunk. She is too young. I think, *No, get away from him. Go back to your tent!*

Drumsticks drop from his hands and he stands blinking at the girl. He takes two steps away from his drum. He shakes his head and sweat swings away, shining in the firelight.

Another step. He and the girl stand practically nose to nose.

He takes her hands and begins swaying with her from side to side as other drummers play on. She moves stiffly at first, looking right and left as if she has lost something, then aligns her face with his and begins to mimic his movement.

For a while they dance with arms supporting each other. The girl begins to smile when their faces move close enough to breathe each other's breath. Their laughter starts slowly, then they fall over each other to the ground, laughing hard. I watch helplessly as they touch skin to skin and their laughter stops.

And I am a bird that flies higher and higher as they lie far below, bodies straining against each other with open mouths, crying out in abandon at the edge of the dusty clearing.

The glob of light and all its noise fades and the sun rises. The girl with brown hair lies alone in the middle of the clearing, eyes staring fixedly at the ground. She stands up slowly, grasps at her torn shift, and stumbles toward a line of tents, feet slapping unevenly on the hard earth.

Someone covers me with a blanket of warm fur.

A deep breath. I open my eyes.

Mother tends a newly kindled fire, smiling to herself in the quiet. Smoke from the fire draws up and out through a hole at the top of the tent.

"I guess my story was not as interesting as I thought." She reaches out a ladle to pour me a cup of warm broth.

"It *was* interesting." I look hard at my mother. "I saw you. And him."

Her hand jerks and some broth spills on my leg.

"I told you. I am a Three Face."

"How much did you see?"

"Too much."

She hands me my cup of broth and ladles a cup for herself. Steam curls over my face. The broth is delicious.

"You have his eyes, you know. The color of leaves and honey and brown in the center. The only person I have ever seen with eyes like his is you."

"What was his name again?"

"Thanillo."

The word lingers in the heavy air of our tent. We both sip our broth and remember.

CHAPTER FOUR

Mother and I have managed to share our morning meal without speaking. I have to get out of the tent.

"I think I will go find Varno. I want to tell him what I saw."

"Did you see Chakka yet? I am sure she has missed you." Mother does not look at me.

Chakka. I had forgotten her.

I step out of the tent and walk toward the forest edge. Something out of my field of vision moves like light shifting on leaves, and suddenly a wild cat with yellowish gray fur and dark markings is standing in front of me. The cat is panting with mouth open, dark pink tongue moving up and back between white fangs that seem too large for the face.

I stand still, feeling the beauty of this wild creature wash through me.

It walks up to me, brushes its tail on my left leg and nips my right shin; I see my skin pulled for an instant between small white incisor teeth. The cat stares up at me, green eyes riveted to my face.

"Hello Chakka. I missed you too." I bend down to hug the compact, muscular body. The thick fur is warm and clean. The cat walks toward the forest, stops, and looks back at me.

"I am coming," I say and it bounds off, stopping again and looking back so I can catch up. I know where I am being led. We have a special rock outcrop in the woods where we go to watch animals and listen to birds. It is near a narrow brook of ice melt tumbling down along fallen boulders. Our secret place.

Chakka reminds me of Father. He started teaching me bird songs and animal tracking from the time I started to walk. He never worried that I spent hours by myself at the edge of the tribal compound, whistling to birds and coaxing squirrels and mice to take morsels of food from my fingers.

One day I heard high-pitched cries in the forest. I followed the sound to a shallow hole under a shrub. There, half buried in dead leaves and soil was a lone speckled wildcat cub. Abandoned? I had a sense that the mother cat was dead. I lifted the cub in my hand for a better look and the wild baby spat and hissed at me. That was it. My heart was stolen.

I remember how everyone stared when I carried the cub through the compound and back to our tent. No one in our tribe likes animals unless they can be eaten.

"Mother, look what I found!" She kept her distance but Father came to look. He smiled at the baby wildcat cupped against my chest, wrapped in a piece of hide torn from my shift.

Mother looked toward Father and waited.

He smiled and began instruction. "The cub needs food. It only has tiny teeth so it cannot eat meat yet. Run and get some milk from Tonna. She is still nursing Lun; she can spare a small amount. We will grind the milk together with some chopped up meat and make a paste. I think the cub will be able to eat that."

He reached over and lifted the cub's tail. "Good, a female. Not as wild as a male."

Father looked over to Mother. "I will ask Tonna for some milk," she said, walking away with a smile.

I tried to rub my face against her fur, but she spat again and backed away against my wrist.

Father continued his teaching. "Make her a cage out of willow sticks so she will not run away. She needs time to get used to us. What will you name her?"

"Name her? I did not think of that." It only took me a second to hear her name in my mind. "Chakka? It reminds me of her pointy teeth and claws."

"Chakka. I like that. She will learn her name quickly and when she gets bigger she will follow you around. That is, if she decides to stay with us."

"What do you mean?"

"She is a wild animal. She may not stay with us once she gets big enough to live on her own. Nothing can keep a wild animal with humans except love," Father said with a smile.

"Then I will tame her with love. She will never go away." It never occurred to me that Chakka would not love me back.

Mother returned with milk, and Father showed me how to use a stone to grind it with meat and a bit of water to make a fine paste. I dipped my finger into the mixture and held it to Chakka's mouth, which was in the middle of producing a tiny roar as my finger moved toward her face.

Then she smelled the food. She seemed interested and touched her brown triangle nose to my finger to sniff. Almost against her will, a coarse pink tongue came from her mouth and rasped up the mix from my finger.

Back and forth, Chakka took the mix from my finger and I dipped it back in for more. Soon it was gone and she was pushing her face against my hand, snuffling loudly.

"I think she needs more," I said. "She is still hungry."

"Let me get some more meat and we will grind it with water for her. I do not want to bother Tonna again." Mother looked away, trying to hide a big smile.

We made more of the meat mixture, and Chakka lapped it up, used to my finger and scent by now. She leaned into my arms and began to vibrate against me with eyes half closed, a bit of pink tongue sticking out of her mouth.

"What is that noise? Is she sick?"

"No, she is telling you she is content," said Father. He did not try hide his smile.

"How do you know all this?" Father smiled again and for a moment he looked like a young boy to me.

"I want to show her to Varno. Can I?" looking up, trying to read Mother's slight frown and Father's bland expression.

"Let her show her friend the cub. Tomorrow." Father said. What I did not know was that tonight he would go to Savvo and let him know we had brought the wild cub into our tent. Some people might not approve, but most would. A wildcat would keep away the insects and vermin that always got into our food.

The next day I brought Varno to our tent to show off the cub.

"How did you find her?" he asked, looking at her with big eyes.

"I heard her crying in the forest, and followed the sound."

"And you were not afraid?" His slanted eyes got even bigger.

"Why would I be?"

Varno frowned. "The cub's mother might have attacked you!"

"I knew she was dead." I said simply.

"You did not!"

But I did. I had seen a quick impression of the mother wildcat lying dead, her throat ripped out by wolves.

"I just knew."

Varno laughed, and put out his finger to try to stroke the hissing cub.

Seeing Chakka now reminds me how happy we used to be.

The fact that I am a Three Face is sinking in. After seeing Mother and that drumming boy at the ritual of the Great Cliff tribe I feel embarrassed. I cannot get the two figures on the ground out of my mind.

But why should I not have seen it? It is the moment I was created. I was meant to see it so I could feel the love that existed between my real father and my mother.

I did not see love.

Thanillo and Mother were friends their whole lives and that night he did not even know who she was.

I begin to feel a red burning in my stomach. I keep seeing Thanillo in his drumming trance. I want to move the story back to the start of the ritual and change the way things turn out.

What good is being a Three Face if I do not have the power to change anything?

I still do not know how Mother came to the Golden Fish tribe. I should go back inside our tent.

"I am back," I blurt out, pushing back the tent flap and ducking my head as I crawl in.

No response, no movement. She is sitting, staring straight ahead, doing nothing. I think, *When was the last time I saw Mother doing nothing?*

I start moving toward her, then pull back.

"I am ready to hear more of the story."

Mother pushes her hair back from her face and looks away. "Are you sure you will be able to stay awake?"

My face feels hot. "I want to hear more."

"All right." Settling into the sitting cushion she reaches for her cup. "More broth?"

"No, I just want to hear what happened."

She takes a deep sip from her cup and sighs. "Where did we leave off?"

My throat and stomach tighten up.

"Oh, I remember, the Spring Dreaming Ritual. It is the first seasonal ceremony of the Great Cliff tribe."

"You call that a ceremony?" I interrupt.

"Are you going to let me tell the story?" Her voice is raised, dark eyes drilling into mine. I look down into my lap. She continues.

"Every year it is the same. The ceremony after the Spring Ritual happens with the next full moon. That is when the Holy One initiates acolytes chosen to become his Holy Followers. This is a high honor. Acolytes assist the Holy One in all things. They study all the ceremonies and commune with the Spirits. One day the next Holy Follower ascends to the station of Holy One.

"Thanillo had always been my best friend, and since the Spring Dreaming Ritual all I thought about was joining with him.

"We all sat in front of our respective tent sites, forming a circle around the center of our encampment. Thanillo and another boy stood in the center. I was so proud that he was chosen to be a Holy Follower. Our lives would be so interesting. I knew nothing of the Spirit world, but I was ready to learn." She takes a long breath and goes on.

"The initiation began with Thanillo and the other boy having all their hair shaved off. Then their old clothes were stripped from their bodies and burned. They were given new robes made of hide sewn with colored beads depicting herbs and drums. With shaved heads and new robes the boys changed right before my eyes."

"Changed? How?"

"The Holy One chanted a prayer and with each word Thanillo stood taller, like he was discovering his purpose. He never looked at me. Not even once." She stopped to clear her voice and take a sip from her cold cup of broth.

She looked straight into my eyes. "I am telling you that when the chant was finished Thanillo was a stranger to me."

I feel stunned by what Mother is saying. How can a chant by a Holy One take away a friend?

"Of course, the only thing that did not change was the color of his eyes. Like leaves, with rays of honey coming out from a dark center. Like your eyes."

I am sick of hearing about my eyes. "Then what happened?"

"The initiation ended and the Holy Followers moved from their parents' tents into the Holy One's tent. I did not see Thanillo much after that. And then *I* started to change."

"Into what?"

Mother gives a quick laugh. "I was tired and hungry all the time. When I went out with the other girls to pick herbs and tubers, I could barely put one foot in front of the other. I would find a spot in the sun, lay my head on my collection bag, and fall asleep. When I woke up all the girls were laughing at me! I felt so stupid. And the hunger! I craved so much meat, my mother and father could barely keep me fed."

"What was wrong with you?"

"Nothing. I was with child. It happened on the night of the Spring Dreaming Ritual with Thanillo."

She was only a girl. It was only a crazy ritual.

"My parents knew right away what was wrong with me, and guessed that something had happened at the ritual. It was not uncommon, and helped nervous young people decide on their mate. Adults took advantage of the Spring Dreaming

Ritual to meet with someone who was not their joined mate. On that one night of the year, there were no restrictions on behavior between men and women. Anything was sanctioned. Anything, that is, except what Thanillo and I did."

"Why was that so different?"

"Thanillo was a part of the Holy One's spiritual entourage now. He would never join, never father children, never have friends again. He would study and master the ways of the Holy One, and someday he might become the next Holy One of the Great Cliff tribe. He certainly could not acknowledge a child with me, an ordinary girl, a no one."

"You were with child. With me!"

"Yes dear."

"What happened then?"

"Mother and Father were angry and humiliated. I was going to bring forth a baby from a forbidden union with a Holy Follower, so I could never join with the father. Either I had to join with another boy from the tribe, or..." She stops talking, hugs herself and looks away.

"Or what?"

"I could leave. Or kill myself to avoid the shame."

"What shame? Everyone *made* you take the drink. I was there. It was not your idea." I see a quick image of the girl staring into a cup and many hands shoving it at her face." I slide over to hug my Mother, to protect her.

"It does not matter now. The Great Cliff tribe has rules like our tribe does. A girl who is with child and cannot join with the father must either find someone else to join with or leave. She cannot be a burden to the tribe. A woman with a young one and nobody to take responsibility for feeding both of them is a burden."

"What about your parents?"

"Father was an older man, and he adhered strictly to tribal laws. He did not want a Holy Follower's denied child in his family. It would be bad luck. He was not much of a provider and barely able to hunt for Mother and me. If I stayed, he would have to feed a young girl with a newborn baby. He did not want that responsibility."

I think about her parents – the grandparents I never knew – and I feel a red pain rising in my stomach. "You were not some stranger. You were their daughter!

"Women are only wanted when they can do work for others," she raises an eyebrow and looks at me.

"What did you do?"

"Mother suggested I leave. I have to admit I thought about killing myself by jumping off the high cliff, but I did not have the courage. If you saw that cliff you would understand."

"You had a whole tribe of people around you. Was there no one else who would join with you?"

"You of all people should understand. I loved *Thanillo*, and I had thought he loved me. I did not want to be joined for the rest of my life to one of the other boys of the tribe. That would have hurt me more than anything else."

I *do* understand. It is how I feel about being a Three Face.

"I made up my mind to leave. I did not say anything, but I think my parents knew. I gathered food during the day, tied it in a hide, and hid it near our tent under a pine shrub. I pretended to go to sleep but instead I waited until the middle of the night when the fires are darkest and everyone is asleep. I crept from the tent, found the food bundle, slung it over my shoulder, and walked out into the no man's land between tribes. I had heard another tribe lived where the land meets the Great Water and started walking down the coast to find them."

I am so proud of my mother. That took courage. I want to hear how she met Father.

"When you found the Golden Fish tribe, did you walk into the compound and say 'hello, here I am?'"

"It does not work that way."

"Why not? Were we *all* savages?"

"Not all of us. But a stranger cannot walk into the inner circle of another tribe. The scouts would stop me, which is exactly what happened. Your father – Ruano – happened to be scouting the day I wandered into Golden Fish territory. I was stumbling along, starving and thirsty, all my food gone. He saw I was young, weak, swollen with a growing baby, and took pity on me. Ruano escorted me into the tribal territory. I had to be presented to The Old One immediately for consideration."

"What does that mean – consideration?"

"I was judged."

Judged. No, we are not savages. Just heartless.

"I was brought into the center of the Golden Fish compound. Apart from the sip of water and bite of food from Ruano, I was given nothing. The whole tribe gathered together in the center of camp sitting around me in a big circle of staring faces.

While Mother is speaking I see the scene. This is getting easier. Her voice recedes to a whisper in the background.

The young girl with brown hair sways weakly while The Old One questions her. I know it is The Old One because of his headdress with the shells over his eyes and his voice like angry stones banging together.

"How have you come to us, girl?"

"I am going to have a child." The whole tribe laughs at the young girl whose thick belly is distended tightly against her skimpy shift. "I had to leave the Great Cliff tribe. I heard there were people here, so I walked."

"Why would you have to leave because you are going to have a child? Did the father not want you?"

The girl hesitates and almost loses her balance. No one moves to help her.

Ruano stands stiffly with proper decorum, but his cheeks tighten and he shifts his weight from one foot to the other. His eyes stay on the girl.

She recovers herself and continues. "I am in love with the boy – the *father* – but he is a Holy Follower of our Holy One. He cannot join."

Whispers and exclamations burst from the crowd. The Old One turns strangely pale under his dark robe and headdress.

"You chose to leave your tribe. Was there no one else in your tribe who would join with you?" Not The Old One, but a kinder voice. Savvo. He was already leader then.

"I am in love with *that* boy, the child's father." The girl raises her chin and looks Savvo in the eye.

Some of the women nod their heads and whisper among themselves.

The Old One is having trouble clearing his throat. He has been pale since the Great Cliff Holy One was mentioned. He puts up one hand for silence, makes a fist and bangs his chest a few times with the other. The crowd quiets immediately.

"Who can say what kind of spirit the unborn may have when its mother is rejected by her own tribe? The strengths and weaknesses, and the effect you and the offspring of a foreign Holy Follower may have on *our* tribe, must all be taken into consideration."

A hum of voices rises again from the crowd of people. It sounds like many feel afraid of Mother and the unborn offspring of a Holy man from another tribe.

Ruano steps into the center of the compound next to the girl and clears his throat. The crowd hushes and The Old One frowns.

"I would address the tribe," he says with his head held high, and looks straight at The Old One. Ruano is a hunter of wild animals and a scout who protects the tribal borders from hostile intruders. He does not seem to be afraid of an old man, no matter the robes or headdress.

His voice is quiet and direct. "This young woman is alone, except for her unborn child. She has traveled far because her own people rejected her. I will not allow that to happen again. If The Old One in his wisdom agrees, I will take her as my mate and we will be joined as members of the Golden Fish tribe. Even if The Old One does not agree, I have made up *my* mind. I *will* join with her." There is a hush in the compound. Ruano adds these final words. "I will join with this woman even if I have to leave the Golden Fish tribe with her and strike out on my own."

I slide easily back to the present. Why was this man not my father instead of some frenzied acolyte? But in every sense except one, he was. I wish he was still here so I could talk to him.

Mother continues the story with feeling. Her cheekbones and nose are flushed, as if she has been crying.

"Ruano saved my life. It took me running away from my own tribe and nearly dying from starvation to discover there is more to life than thinking you love someone. There is knowing someone, respecting them, and accepting their goodness given from the heart. Then true love can grow."

My mother stops speaking; she looks tired but relaxed. And then one more sentence, "Ruano and I were joined and you were born soon after, and the world became a bright place for me every day since that day."

"Thank you for telling me these things," is all I can think to say. It is not much, but I mean it. I feel very tired. Traveling out of my body into another time has exhausted me.

"Rest now. We can decide in the morning what to do about your visions."

"What if The Old One does not want me to follow my visions? I do not want to have to stand in the middle of the tribe and be under consideration like you were. I will just go. I know now what to do."

Mother's face, which had been soft and sleepy but happy, is now sharply attentive. "What *will* you do?"

"I will go to the tribe of the Great Cliff to find my birth father – Thanillo – with the eyes like mine. He is probably the tribal Holy One by now. I will present myself to him. When he sees me he will have to acknowledge I am his daughter."

CHAPTER FIVE

I fall into a deep sleep. After hearing my mother's story about our life and my father Thanillo, I am not ready for much more than passing into sleep to recharge my body and mind. I fall into a dark, empty place.

I have the most vivid dream of my life.

My feet are callused like ram's horn from treading barefoot along the rutted path that runs alongside the cliffs of the Great Water. It is summer and the water birds dive into the surf, coming up with silvery fish in their beaks. Other birds with large black wings cut sharply right and left between the water birds, trying to scare them into dropping their catch. When the water birds open their beaks to squawk the shining fish fall and the black winged birds, with supreme grace and agility, twist downward to grab the fish before they hit the water.

I watch the birds and walk along, listening to my feet slap out a satisfying rhythm on the hard path. There is nothing to think about as I nibble some pine nuts stored in a pliable skin pouch hanging across my body, and enjoy the scent of herbs growing in the hot sun, fed only with moisture rising up from the Great Water.

And then, a feeling of being watched. Stalked. Is it an animal? There are no strange odors, only the overpowering scent of herbs and the Great Water. Waves boom against the cliffs on my left. The land on my right is covered in stiff brush and grass beating in the air. Nothing else will grow up here where wind and salt from the Great Water eat into the earth day and night.

This is a land of stark beauty with nowhere to hide.

The cliff offers only empty air and a quick death on the boulders below.

These thoughts travel through me in a split second. I have no route of escape, no choice but to meet whatever it is head on. I breathe deeply and take one step, another step, and then another, until I am walking deliberately along the path, alert to every air current, sound and smell that is different from the mist rising from the Great Water.

Now I see it. Many paces ahead a human figure faces toward me as if waiting. It becomes more defined with each step I take until I see a man with shaven head wearing a beaded white robe. I want to see his features more clearly.

Soon I am five paces from the white-robed shaven head man and still he has not moved a muscle. Symbols are etched into his cheeks and forehead with a dark pigment. I do not recognize them; they must have a Spirit meaning. While his face is unremarkable, his eyes grab me somewhere near my heart – greenish brown eyes with gold flecks. Suddenly the man reaches out with hands that change into claws. His arms become long and snake swiftly out toward me. I have no time to react!

I wake with a huge intake of air, sit upright, and stare into darkness. The fire is down to dying embers. Mother is asleep on the other side of the hearth. My heart pounds loudly and deep breaths rasp into my lungs.

I think Mother must be able to hear my heart pounding, but she sleeps peacefully.

That was more than a dream, it was a vision. Did it show my future? Will I leave the Golden Fish tribe in search of my birth father, Thanillo? That is what I said to Mother after she told me our story. I thought she looked frightened, as if leaving could be dangerous.

If The Old One does not accept my vision quest, there is no place for me in the Golden Fish tribe.

I know the dream man on the path is Thanillo. What do the claw hands mean?

Why did I not dream about Ruano, my *true* father. He was the tribe's best scout and hunter and he loved Mother and me. Why can I not have another chance to speak to him, a true man, instead of fake men in long robes who think they can decide people's fates? What could be more of a man's role than loving a family and being kind to other people? Now I will never have a family. I do not *choose* to be a Three Face. My visions are frightening. I need to sleep, not to sit up thinking about strangers with snake arms.

Since I am awake I guess I should think about the next day and what it will bring. What exactly is going to happen?

I think Mother will go to The Old One and Savvo and tell them I have returned. She will say something about me not having the same kind of visions as the rest of the girls.

Savvo will listen and be understanding of whatever my vision quest showed to me, but I do not need to wonder how The Old One will react. He will be quick to find fault and make me into an outcast.

The Old One has never liked me. Why should he? When he told us stories in Learning Circle, I thought I was too smart to listen. The story where the Great Water rises to cover our tribal land. The one where the sun turns black with a halo of light around it. The cold time when a mountain of ice grows over the land. The story of the Three Face who turns into a wolf and runs through the forest together with the stag. Back then I knew his stories were fake. I could not help giggling when he gestured and swayed in his long robes, trying to bring them to life.

Now that I have seen my own visions I know The Old One's stories are true. But my past actions cannot be changed.

The Old One and Savvo will decide to bring me and my vision quest before the tribe for consideration.

Will they ostracize Mother for having a strange daughter with strange eyes who came from a strange tribe?

Will The Old One say my visions mean I need to go back to the Great Cliff tribe? I will have to agree. That is what I think my visions mean.

I sit up straight in the tent imagining tomorrow's tribal meeting. I will be judged, like Mother was. My future will be up for consideration by people who do not know me.

I do not want to be judged! Whatever wrong I have done, I am not going to let The Old One punish me in front of Savvo and the rest of the tribe.

My hands take on a life of their own, pulling off stale clothes, reaching out for a clean shift and a shawl, raking through the loose ends of hair falling in my face.

I crawl out of our tent and stand with my head thrown back to find my favorite stars in the black sky. The night is perfect, clear and not too chilly.

The Old One's tent is situated in a powerful position beside Savvo's tent. Although it stands apart from the others, a blind person could find it by the aroma. Too many steeping herbal potions, too many ritual burnings of magical plants.

I hesitate outside the tent opening and listen; there is movement inside. The Old One awake already, kindling his cook fire for morning tea?

"Identify yourself," drones the gravelly voice.

I thought I was being quiet. "It is Astara."

"You have come." Is he expecting me?

"May I speak with you?"

"Enter."

I push back the tent flap with two fingers and poke my head inside. The smell of burning dung and potent herbs hits my face and I cough spasmodically.

Still coughing I climb in, turn and sit to face him, and am surprised that instead of looking into The Old One's eyes, I am looking at a row of cowrie shells hanging from red leather thongs. He is wearing his headdress. Does he sleep in it?

The headdress catches me off guard. "I want to speak about my vision quest. I do not want to be judged in front of the tribe!" I think, *If I confront him here in private, The Old One may speak honestly with me.*

The voice that comes out of his mouth is harsh. "You burst into my tent, do not greet me with proper respect, and now you do not want to be judged. As usual you are thinking only of yourself instead of showing humility and dignity."

"I am *not* thinking only…"

He cuts me off. "I have been watching you since before you were born. When my name was still Fulano, long before I was The Old One, you invaded my dreams."

I feel my face getting hot. Did I hear right?

"I saw your eyes, the color of forest and honey, eyes of a Three Face, a Spirit talker, animal shifter. I did not understand the meaning then."

"You have known all along that I am a Three Face? If you know my vision is real, why must my vision be 'judged'?

He practically spits out the words. "Because you are disrespectful. You laugh at my teachings in Learning Circle. You show no inclination to study. You never had an interest in the lore of the Three Face but now, out of nowhere, you want to *be* a Three Face!"

I hunch my head down between my shoulders. I did laugh at him. Always so dirty looking, always hiding his eyes. If he was not so haughty when he shared his teachings with us, they would seem more real. But now I understand him, and I want to tell him so.

"I was wrong to laugh at the stories, but I have changed and now I want to learn everyth..."

"*Stop speaking girl!*" A thick stench of breath hits me in the face. "You want, you want! What *you* want does not concern me!"

My heart is pounding now. People can change. Thanillo did. "I want to learn what you know. I am different since my vision quest." I speak quickly so he cannot cut me off.

"What makes you think I will let you take away my position within the tribe by recognizing you as a Three Face? Have you ever been a serious person? Have you concerned yourself with Spirit? *No!* Just the opposite. I do not understand why Spirit would allow such an unworthy girl to be a Three Face, but it is not my place to question. All I know is that there will be no Three Face woman in *my* tribe!"

"Why am I being denied a chance to study? You cannot stop me from being what I am!"

"You can study to be a Three Face someplace else. Or you can forget your visions and become a normal woman of this tribe. It will be your choice."

He turns his back to me. My audience with The Old One is over.

"I cannot forget my visions," I say to the dark robe. "I have already seen too much."

He exhales in a low moan, but does not move or speak.

I back out of his tent and walk away from the area as fast as I can. My head is tingling and my eyes sting.

The Old One dreamed about me before I was born! What is the story behind my eyes?

The grey light of dawn makes the tents look like strange humped animals in the humid air. I find our tent and slide in quietly.

"Where have you been?" Mother says softly.

"For a walk," I say, smiling as if everything is normal. "I thought you would be asleep."

"I could not sleep. I dreamed about Ruano. Losing him was the first sign my life was turning in the wrong direction."

I do not want to remember how my father Ruano was killed on the winter hunt two seasons ago. But now it all comes rushing back with the strength of a gale force wind.

It was the first time the men of the tribe had gone hunting so far away. Ruano and the other scouts had gone over the terrain on summer expedition. But this was the first time the Golden Fish hunters would venture so far on a winter hunt. Large elks or boars with spiky hair and tusks would make better quarry than the small deer, pigs and pheasant they normally hunted. These smaller animals were in abundance within the tribe's territory, but the larger game would feed more people and the hides, bones and tusks were valuable for clothing, tents, weapons, ornaments, and carvings. No one understood that the big game could be so dangerous.

Ruano led the charge, running alongside a huge and wily boar, when the animal unexpectedly veered to the right. A curved tusk sliced into Ruano, sweeping him backward and off his feet.

One moment a strong and vital man ran and readied his spear, the next he sailed through the air trailing a veil of blood behind him. His body slammed full force against the trunk of a massive tree, snapping his head backward and cracking his skull against the trunk. He died instantly, covered in blood.

The chase went on frantically, the hunting party avenging Ruano's death by killing the old boar, but nothing could bring back life. Instead of twelve men carrying the spoils home in triumph to the tribe, eleven men carried butchered animals, hides, tusks, and the body of Ruano in silence through the forest.

As if it was yesterday, I see the hunters materialize out of the trees and trudge over the hill, dragging heavy loads on wooden litters behind them. The men's feet seem to slow as they approach the tribal compound.

I have been waiting for them, excited to see Father and hear his stories of the hunt. I run out to the forest edge to meet them, trying to spot him among the hunters.

They look away from me but I see their tears and hear their silence. Then I see the wrapped body and I know who it is. I am only eight years and some months at the time and do not fully understand that something could happen to Father.

Mother keeps her decorum and waits for the men to relate the story of what happened. No one ever addresses her directly to explain how Ruano lost his life.

Instead, according to tribal protocol, over the communal fire the hunters relate to the entire tribe how Ruano was killed by the giant boar. The huge beast is one of the butchered animals brought back from the hunt. The right tusk still bears Ruano's blood, bringing a sharp reality to the already powerful story. People cry out in sympathy and horror as the story is told.

Mother sits as still as stone, her face a mask. I remember following her example, sitting like a mature woman, staring straight ahead, holding my mother's hand.

Everyone waits to see how we will carry ourselves. All those years ago Mother had been accepted into the tribe. She was treated cordially after Ruano joined with her, but now people wait for some lapse in composure and strength, something to indicate that she is less than equal to a Golden Fish woman. That night she proves she belongs here.

After Ruano's death, when the hunters go out there is no meat coming home to us. Mother refuses to be a burden to the other families and does not ask for help.

We will soon starve without meat, so I watch the boys play at hunting in order to learn what to do. Varno shows me how to trap and kill small animals such as birds, rabbits and squirrels; I am already the best at catching fish in my hands. I become a hunter so that we can sustain ourselves while keeping our pride and placement within the tribe.

I am happy to feed Mother and me now that Father is gone, but I hate killing the animals that used to be my friends.

I love animals. The squirrels and birds that used to entertain me might now become my victims. I try to concentrate on killing game birds rather than any of 'my' squirrels, but it is hard to tell one squirrel from another. I begin to mentally catalog the markings on each animal so I will recognize those I have tamed. One has a shorter tail, probably bitten off when a hawk or wildcat tried to catch it. Another has a fuller, reddish tail. Still another is dark with white spots on its sides – that one is easy to tell apart from the others. I do not want to think of these animals as food; they are my friends.

Except for Varno, sometimes they are the only friends I have.

If I acted like all the other girls in the tribe, the fact that Mother was an outsider would have easily been overlooked. Our people are happy and industrious, and have better things to do than find differences in each other. But I know I have always been uncomfortably different. Even though everyone tried to look the other way I was unlike anyone else in the tribe, even my own Mother.

I jar myself away from these memories. No sense in looking back now. Tomorrow I will be brought before The Old One and the members of the tribe for 'consideration' and judgment like Mother was all those years ago. They will listen to my visions and decide whether I will be allowed to continue as a Three Face within the framework of the tribe, or forced to adhere to the visions of the other girls and join with a boy of the tribe.

Or perhaps I will simply be sent away to find my destiny with another tribe, or with death.

CHAPTER SIX

"We need to bathe and put on clean clothes before we go to Savvo and The Old One," Mother says, like it is an ordinary day.

"Give me a minute." I rummage through my shifts to find one that looks good enough. I think the monthly flow is finished, but put my hand down between my legs and move my fingers around to see if they come out with blood. Almost gone. A bath in the Great Water will take away the last of it.

I find a clean shift and grab a washing cake made of boiled fat and wood ash so I can clean my hair. I have been gone a few days sleeping in the forest, but it is more likely to get lice from people. I have not been near any people except for Mother and The Old One. Lice can live on anyone. That is why Mother rinses our tent and bedding in the Waters often, and lets them dry in the hot sun and wind. Lice do not like sun and wind.

I am fairly certain The Old One does not air out his bedding. Thoughts of him occupy me as I crawl out of our tent.

The Old One wears a dark brown elk skin robe that starts at his shoulders and ends at his dusty, cracked feet. The robe looks scratchy and stiff, as if when it was tanned somebody left some of the flesh and hairs attached because they did not like him, and did not want to put in the effort to tan the hides for his robe properly. Or perhaps it is part of the aura of a Holy person. They do not need soft robes and beautiful clothes. Their appearance should be harsh and jarring to convey the strength it takes to live with the Spirits. In this The Old One succeeds.

The dark robe covers The Old One's body and he wears a headdress of dark hide, glossy with age and molded to fit his head exactly. Strips of dyed red leather strung with golden cowrie shells hang in a row along the front of the headdress, screening The Old One's eyes. Stiffly molded hides cover the soles of his feet; he is the only one in the tribe to wear foot coverings. He does not do much walking so the soles of his feet must be tender from lack of use. The Old One smells old if you get too close, probably from all the herbs and potions he uses to help him see the past and the future. The air around his tent maintains a strong odor of dung and vegetable matter from his hearth and the drying herbs and seeds he uses in his rituals. Nobody is supposed to come near his tent, and nobody wants to because of the smell.

The only visible part of The Old One's face is the lower half of his nose, his mouth, and his chin. The skin is dark as if tanned by the sun, but he rarely leaves his tent and never sits in the sunshine so I wonder how he got that way. I do not remember seeing him smile, ever, but when he speaks you can see his teeth. For one who is supposed to be so old, his teeth look strong and straight. They are brownish, probably from all the potions he drinks and the strong leaves he smokes. The Old One may be old but he does not seem frail. He will probably live forever.

"Astara! Time to bathe. Stop fussing!" Mother calls from beyond the tent. She is already on the path toward the Great Water.

"Coming!" I snatch up a shift and the washing patty and start down the sandy path toward the sea. A furry blur catches up to my feet, reaches out with a quick paw, then runs back into the scrub along the path.

"Chakka! Come here girl!" I call. The wildcat entices me to play, darting back and forth across the path, tail curved up and then downward. She has seven seasons, and is strong and well able to catch her own food. She stays in the forest near our tent during the day, and in the evening comes into the compound like she owns it, picking her way through all the people until she finds me. Then she circles a few times and falls asleep in my lap as we all sit by the fire sharing our stories of the day.

"I have to go down to the Water now," I tell her. I fully believe she understands every word I say. "We can play later. I know you do not like the sand and water in your fur."

She bounds off into the brush once more with a happy meow sound. I am so glad I saw her again. I hope that if I have to leave, Chakka will follow me to wherever I go.

The waves rush up to the shore, hissing over stones and shells whose black, gold and orange colors are magnified by the clear water. Back and forth the water goes, in and out, pulling the stones and shells with it, tumbling and turning up new colors and shapes with every wave. The Great Water is the only constant I have known in my life, apart from Mother, the only thing that is always moving but always there, comforting and clean, a giver of life.

The tide laps at my feet. Mother is already out beyond the first breakers, dunking her head to rinse her hair under the water. She bobs up, smiles and waves.

I push through the waves to join her. The water feels cold at first. It is early and the sun is not yet fully up in the sky, but I know the day will become hot and dry. With that in mind the cold water feels good. I am encrusted with dirt from the last few days of sleeping in the forest and hiking back to the tribe. And I cannot wait to clean my hair. I envision the half-covered face of The Old One and dunk my head quickly, gripping the washing patty with my fingernails and rubbing it over my hair until I feel suds.

Later Mother will comb and braid my hair so I look presentable for my judgment. I am not nervous. I know how The Old One will vote, and although Savvo will speak for me I think the rest of the tribe is afraid of The Old One. Once they hear my visions, they will not want me around. They will be afraid of me too.

I push out nearer to Mother and dunk myself under the waves. Even though the water is salty I lather up and scrub away all the dirt and worry of the past few days. I will adjust quickly to taking care of myself if I have to leave, but what about Mother? Who will take care of her if she stays behind with the tribe? I want to ask her, but she is dunking and smiling and I do not know how to bring it up.

She goes below the water's surface then pops up right beside me a moment later, her frizzy hair plastered down over her head. We both laugh as she splashes water in my face. "Which shift are you going to wear?" she shouts over the constantly moving water, as if we were going for an everyday stroll along the beach.

"The tan one with red and blue beads around the neck. It has sleeves, which I think will make me look like any other girl of the tribe." The sleeves hide my shoulders, strong like a boy's from climbing trees and cliffs.

"That one is a good choice," she answers, smiling and looking away.

I feel a tightness inside my belly. Why is she acting like this judgment is nothing? We should be planning. "What will you do if the tribe decides I should leave?"

I dunk my head under the water so I do not have to see the sad look on her face.

I bob up again, sluicing water off my face and hair. Mother speaks over the rush of waves, "I do not know. I have been trying to believe that The Old One and Savvo will find your visions acceptable, and that you will be treated the same as a boy would be if he had the same visions. That will be my argument to The Old One and the tribe."

"It is a good point. I have been thinking that I will be cast out, and so it did not occur to me to come up with an argument in my favor." I feel excited by these new thoughts. A wave somewhat larger than the others comes unexpectedly and slaps me down under the water. I come up laughing and sputtering. "My visions should be as good as a boy's."

"That is what I am trying to say. They show you do not fall into any one category. A new category must be created for you. I am sure that Savvo sees it the same way I do."

I lather my hair again as a swell floats my feet away from the sandy sea bottom. "There is already a category for me: I am a Three Face. I am sure Savvo will agree, but he is easy to talk to and these things do not mean so much to him. What about The Old One? You know he has always hated me."

"The Old One is afraid of you. He was afraid of you before you were born." I remember The Old One's dream, back when he was Fulano. Does she know about that?

"But *why*? I do not understand why." I try to wave my arms but they are held by the water. The tide is rising and my feet barely touch the bottom now.

Mother continues. "By now Thanillo is probably the spiritual leader of the Great Cliff tribe. He probably has many rituals and visions behind him. And now you, his true daughter, are having visions too. It certainly looks like you are following in his footsteps and you are a woman, which makes you more powerful by far than any man."

The words sink in. A woman more powerful than a man? I have never heard that before. Women are always doing what men tell them to do. They have specific roles to fulfill within the tribe. If they do not follow the roles they can be punished, or ostracized. How can they be more powerful than men? Unless there is a secret nobody talks about. I never understood until now that women are *so* powerful men have felt compelled to give them many rules to follow so they will spend a lot of their energy fitting in. All the rules are there not because women are weak and need to be told what to do, but because women are so strong.

"You think The Old One is afraid that my woman Spirit medicine is stronger than his medicine and that he will be pushed aside by me?" I am finished washing my hair now. I dunk a few more times to make sure the suds are rinsed out completely. Who knows when I will have another chance to bathe once they cast me out. I am certain they will, no matter what Mother says. The Old One will find a way to get rid of me.

"Come out of the water. We need to dry off and get ready for the judgment with Savvo and The Old One." Mother looks back over her shoulder as she slogs past me through the surf that drags at our legs along with shell and stone. "Yes, he is afraid your medicine is stronger."

I catch up to her and continue, "Do not worry about *me*. What will *you* do if I am cast out of the tribe? Are you going to stay here, or are you coming with me?" I look sideways at her through wet tangles of hair. She looks frightened. She has certainly thought about this already. I cannot be the only one who sees this as the real question of the day.

She does not answer. She walks ahead of me, up toward the path that leads back to the compound and our tent. "I am going to dry myself down here in the sun, remember? I brought my shift so I can get dressed down here by the water. Mother?"

She keeps walking like she does not hear me. Did I say something wrong? I run after her, catching up easily as she walks slowly up to the path through deep sand.

"Wait! Stop walking!"

She spins around, face wet from crying.

"I told you the story of my life. Our life. I cannot go back to the Great Cliff tribe. I would not be welcome. And I *cannot* see Thanillo again."

"I hate making you cry. I will be fine on my own."

She wipes at her face and tries to smile. "I know. We should get ready. I still have to plait your hair. We want to look perfect when we go before Savvo and The Old One."

Who cares what I look like? The reality of leaving Mother behind is sinking into my mind and spirit. How will she live? Who will look after her? Savvo? More and more I feel this is not my tribe. These are not our people. I cannot trust them to take care of my mother. The only reason they took her in is because Ruano stood up for her and joined with her. Otherwise they would have sent her away to find another tribe, or to die trying.

I trail after her, picking up my shift and pushing unruly hair out of my face. It is already drying in the rising heat of the day.

"Will you plait my hair for me now?" The simplicity of the request strikes me and I feel tears coming to my eyes. How many more times will I be able to ask my mother to plait my hair?

She turns to look at me, as if memorizing my appearance.

"Let me comb out the hair so it does not tangle, and then I will make a braid, one down your back I think – no?" she says gently, pushing back the hair from my face so she can look into my strange eyes. How can she look at me and not be sad?

"If only your eyes had been blue like other babies when you were born, The Old One would have accepted you." She lifts her arms to comb out my hair and I smell the fresh aromas of cool water and clean skin. "The Old One knows that your eyes are the color of power. I think he knows more about Thanillo than he lets on.

"When he came to bless you, he saw your eyes and started chanting special prayers right away. His face, what I could see of it, became grey as ash when he saw you that first time. For a year The Old One could not look at you. He was afraid but I do not know why."

Something breaks inside me and I am flooded with anger at what is happening to us. What have we done to deserve all this pain? Nothing. I was born with different eyes. So what? Mother came from another tribe. So what? My birth father is probably the Holy One of the Great Cliff tribe by now. So what? Why not simply be who we are and live?

"We should finish getting dressed. The judgment will start soon. I want to see The Old One squirm when he sees me. I want everyone to know that he is afraid of me."

"Whatever our fate, we are ready," says Mother. She looks more composed now that she has braided my hair and my shift is on straight and we are clean from the Great Water. I tell myself that nothing cleanses like the Great Water.

༺༻

We walk over to Savvo's tent and stand outside. Mother wants to speak with the tribe's Leader before speaking with The Old One, or facing a judging tribunal. She is counting on Savvo diverting the whole question simply by saying that my vision quest is as valid as everyone else's. I am curious to hear what Savvo says, but his opinion will always be second to The Old One.

Savvo steps out of his tent. He wears a formal shirt decorated with beads and porcupine quills. "Welcome Orana. Welcome Astara. What is the purpose of your visit today?"

As if he does not know. I have never seen Savvo so formal. All my life I have been running in and out of the Leader's tent with my best friend Varno, his son. We never had to greet each other like this.

Mother begins.

"Greetings Savvo. As you know, recently my daughter Astara underwent the Girls' Coming of Age vision quest. What she saw was unexpected, she became disoriented and ran off in fear, but she has returned to our tribe. Will you listen to Astara's visions before The Old One or the tribe hear them? I am hoping when she tells you about them you will agree they should be given the same treatment as everyone else's, even though they may not be the kind of visions girls are expected to have." Mother looks hard into Savvo's face, willing him to listen.

"Astara, child of the Golden Fish tribe, what did you see during the Girls' Coming of Age Ritual?" I see I have to be formal like he is. Keeping my composure and speaking in the same words as the Leader is an important part of the proceedings.

"Thank you for hearing me, Savvo, Leader of the Golden Fish tribe. On my vision quest I saw myself standing before the Great Water wearing a honey-colored robe sewn with designs in beads of many colors. There was a storm and rain drenched everything around me, but my robes were dry. The dolphins and fish of the sea rose up to see me, and the clouds parted for the sun to shine where I stood. I was Astara, but I was not a girl anymore – or a boy. I was something in between."

"Most interesting. Go on."

"I did not see a joining for myself. I lived alone in a cave among animals. I slept beside the wolf and wildcat. Birds came down from the branches to share their songs. I mixed strong potions from plants and spoke with the Spirits."

Savvo does not speak but only studies me intently at I speak.

"My path had no mate or children or joining. Members of many tribes came to me for counsel which I gave directly from the wisdom of the Spirits. I was skilled in the herbal arts and healed pain, mended broken bones, provided antidotes for scorpion and snake bites. Sometimes I was a stag running in the forest beside the wolf and wildcat."

"I am man, woman and animal all rolled into one. I am a Three Face. Those words for who I am came to me in my vision, but The Old One taught us about the Tree Face in Learning Circle."

Savvo waits for more. Is that not enough? When I remain silent, he continues.

"I can see why you were frightened after your vision quest. It is very different from what is expected for girls. Very interesting. Orana, what do you propose?"

Mother draws herself up with confidence. "I have always respected and been comfortable with your leadership. Your decisions with regard to me have always been kind, generous and wise. I ask that you take Astara's visions seriously. It is true that girls – or even most boys – do not have visions like hers, but the other children are not my Astara.

"She has many talents. She has been different from the day she was born. We all saw her risk injury to save Lun from the fire, while the rest of us froze. My daughter did not have to think, she acted. Her instincts are true. She will bring us good luck if she is allowed to follow her natural inclinations. I beg you to consider that the Golden Fish tribe may benefit from letting Astara blossom into a...Three Face...while living with us.

"Let her become an acolyte of The Old One. Let her vision be used for the good of the tribe. If she is made to leave us my daughter will not simply disappear. She will live on to benefit rival tribes, or start a tribe of her own. Why not allow her to stay here and benefit us? Please." Her voice breaks with her last word.

Savvo sits listening like a rock listens when the grass taps against it in the wind.

Everything is quiet except for the sigh of leaves moving in the breeze. I cannot read Savvo's face but I read Mother's; she is bereft.

The silence is too long; I speak up.

"Savvo, what do you think of my visions?"

He sighs. "I want everyone who is part of the tribe to stay here. Orana, since you came to us you have always followed our laws. You have become one of us. Astara, you were conceived in another tribe but you were born here. This is your home. I am not concerned with your differences. But there are some people who are." He stops and looks toward The One One's tent.

The red burning begins in my stomach, and I shake my shoulders and tap my foot to make it stop. My mouth speaks to Savvo before I can stop it.

"So by 'some people', who do you mean? The rest of the tribe? The girls of the tribe? The Grandmothers? Or one person – The Old One? Is that who we are taking about now? Can I stay here, or do I have to go?"

"Astara! Remember who you are speaking to! Savvo is Leader of the tribe, not you!" Mother raises her voice and her nostrils flare.

Savvo laughs, breaking the tension. Smiling broadly, he opens his arms to both of us. "Come, come, I am not used to hearing about visions like yours. Especially so early in the morning! Astara, I intend to speak in your favor at the judging tribunal. It is the only chance to convince The Old One to allow you to stay with the tribe. He is not well disposed toward letting you stay. He is wary of you. He saw your difference long before you had your visions. He sees visions of his own. The Old One has much power. He will not be easy to sway, but I can try."

That does not sound too encouraging but Savvo wants to help me. It is better to have the Leader on my side than not. Mother reaches her hand out and grabs Savvo's arm.

"You have known us for many years. Ruano was your friend. You have seen Astara and Varno playing together since they were children. Please keep us in your heart when you speak at the tribunal."

"I know you are afraid, but nobody is trying to harm you or Astara."

"What will happen if The Old One sends Astara away? The open road is full of dangers. Look at her. She is just a young girl! *Please.* Do not allow The Old One to send her away. Sending her away could be the end of her life," Mother says with finality. She is pleading, but with a proud inner fire shining brightly.

"I understand," Savvo says, and I believe him. "I have no control over The Old One. If he makes a decision that Astara must leave the tribe, I will have to go along with it. But I can send some of the young men to accompany her on her journey, to help keep her safe."

"It sounds good," I jump in quickly, "but who is going to want to leave the tribe when joining ceremony is coming? All the young men want to join with the young women and start families. Who will want to come with me on a journey?"

"I know Varno will want to come," Savvo says without hesitation.

"I thought Tunnara saw herself joined with Varno. I am sure he will not want to miss *that!*" I think I just snorted when I spoke.

"Everyone heard about Tunnara's vision. But I do not believe Varno will mind missing that joining in order to travel to new lands with his best friend. If he cannot join with you, at least he can be with you and share in your adventures."

I want to hug Savvo but I do not think it would be appropriate so I stop myself. "I hope you are right, my Leader." I feel humbled before another human being for the first time in my life.

"I know I am right. I know my son." He looks at us with a slight smile.

Mother has tears in her eyes again, but seems calmer than she was down at the water this morning. Savvo's promise of Varno as my traveling companion may have quelled her worst fears. It has quelled mine.

"Where is The Old One?" I say. Speaking to him is the only thing left to do. I am afraid, but a part of me is wildly happy to have a final confrontation. This has been steeping inside me since the day I was born.

CHAPTER SEVEN

Savvo opens the flap of his tent for Mother and me. I stumble out, blinded by mid-morning light. The entire tribe has gathered in a ring around the center of the compound murmuring loudly, but they immediately get quiet when they see us. I thought we were supposed to meet privately with The Old One and Savvo before the judging tribunal. Why are all these people here? I look quickly up at Savvo as he guides me with a big hand on my shoulder toward The Old One's tent.

Before I can take another step, the Old One opens his tent flap and emerges into the light. He looks like a piece of driftwood that rolled around in the surf all night, and was tossed up on the beach covered with seaweed and sand. His dark robe is dank and smells a lot like seaweed even from this distance. Savvo grabs my shoulder hard to stop me from moving forward. He whispers, "The Old One will beckon us when he is ready."

I am thrown off. This meeting was *supposed* to be private, but I can see that Savvo is right: we have no control over The Old One. He will do things his own way.

The Old One stares at the three of us without speaking. I try to look at his face but it is hard to see because so much of it is covered.

He wears his usual headdress of stiff molded leather, and the screen of red leather thongs strung with cowrie shells hangs straight down over his eyes. His long nose sticks out below the line of shells, dark skinned and large; I think I see a lot of bristly hair sticking out. He has a face as leathery as the headdress. The Old One is magic, so it is possible the headdress and his skin have grown into one. He does not appear to have any hair under the headdress, so at least that is one part of him that cannot be dirty. The Old One is rarely seen outside of his tent, but I think if his magical powers were real he would find a time in the middle of the night to sneak down to the beach and rinse off when no one was looking.

The long robe is stiff with age and has a polished look. The residue of years sitting before a dung fire and burning sage covers the front of the garment. I cannot see the back from where I stand, but I would not be surprised to see it several shades lighter and cleaner.

Even under the smoky sheen, the beadwork on the front of the robe is spectacular. A central medallion of turquoise and coral beads is sewn into the robe below the collar. Women of the tribe chosen for superior skill have created all the beadwork on The Old One's robe. There are depictions of animals, stars, sun and moon, as well as a chest plate made of sea urchin spines that protects his heart from evil spirits.

He carries a long straight staff made of the hardened flower stalk of the rosette plant that grows high on the cliffs overlooking the Great Water. A simple but powerful decoration of five eagle feathers tied with a red leather thong tops off the staff. His twisted right hand grasps the staff, and the skin on his wrist and forearm is dark and ridged like a weathered pine. The fingernails are yellow and striated like the horn of an old ram, and red ochre stains the cracks in his fingertips. The Old One's feet are showing today, dark skin and hard nails smeared with more red ochre. He opens his mouth to speak, and before the words come out I glimpse strong brown teeth like those of an elk.

I am happy to stay this far away from The Old One. I feel his strong spirit reaching out for me like the clawed hands in my dream. It seems to me the smell of him is a seepage of anger and despair over all the things he believes he has given up because he chose to dedicate himself to the life of a holy man. He does not seem light and wise to me. He stands tall but his shoulders are slightly stooped as though he carries a heavy weight, though all he wears is his robe.

I slit my eyes sideways to see how Mother is, not daring to move a muscle, but making sure I face head-on toward The Old One. Mother is staring evenly at the tribe's Holy Man with her head high and back straight, but her chest moves up and down quickly and her hands tremble slightly.

Savvo's voice shatters my thoughts, and moves like a wave through me. The judging tribunal has begun. "Old One, Father of the Great Water tribe, Wisdom Talker, Rainmaker, Holy Old One of the Golden Fish tribe, I come before you today to request an audience for Orana and Astara."

Savvo speaks each word clearly and separately. The weight of his leadership is behind that greeting and it moves out into the hot air toward The Old One like a thick grey cloud that may carry thunder but is moving quietly for now. "The girl Astara has completed her vision quest at the Girls' Coming of Age Rite. Since she did not see the usual path of a woman of the Golden Fish tribe, she humbly requests your permission to follow the vision that was given to her."

The Old One does not move and takes his time to look at each of us. First Mother. He takes her into those eyes that none of us can see, he digests her spirit and spits out the husk of her, back to where she is standing. I see her legs quake under his life-grabbing gaze, but she remains standing with head held high, and does not look away. He sees her strength and resolve and barely smiles, but I catch his expression.

I cannot see The Old One's eyes shift, but the cowrie screen shakes back and forth as he inclines his head toward Savvo. The two stare eye to eye – or eye to shell – and Savvo's expression does not change. Anyone can see he is not afraid of this old man, but he respects him. I can almost see the place where they meet to feel the other's strength like a man feels his way along the wall of a dark cave.

"Savvo," the deep voice snakes up my spine, "you have brought the defiant young girl and her unfortunate mother to speak with me."

Any murmur from the tribe has stopped completely. A warm breeze thumps The Old One's tent, and the weightless song of a sparrow floats like a guardian of the still forest beyond the compound.

The heat of the sun moves to the strength of middle day, slides from behind the trees, and covers me in sudden robes of warmth. The hard voice grapples up from the old throat again, shattering the reverie. "Young woman, you come before me boldly, as ever. You were given the blessing of the Girls' Coming of Age Rite, and yet you have not changed. You have always been disrespectful and wayward." His words are meant to cut and harm me, but I am covered by the warmth of the sun and stand with my chin up, inclined in his direction. His words sound like the heavy spume of an old man who feels his mortality.

My thoughts shock me. I should be falling on the ground before The Old One, crying and begging forgiveness for my childish transgressions. I know I have been disrespectful at times, but I am not sorry.

He watches me carefully, or rather the cowrie shells swing toward me, hairy nostrils flaring, claw hand tightening on the staff while the eagle feathers stir soundlessly.

"Speak girl. You have come here to tell me something you *think* you saw during your vision quest. I am waiting now to hear your voice." There is an impatience to him, and something else. What is it? I see it, like a deer stopping to sniff the air while the wolf stalks, like a squirrel deciding to stay or run while the hawk soars beyond seeing.

I feel it. The Old One is afraid. He knows that another like me lives, my birth father Thanillo, Holy

One of the Great Cliff tribe. What will happen if he and I should meet and join forces? The Old One runs that risk if he casts me out of the Golden Fish tribe.

I see an image of an old man grasping at thoughts, like a man who falls over a cliff grasps at loose branches and dusty stones. He will not let me take away his life and power within this tribe. He could kill me – he wants to – but he must find another way.

He finds a thought to grasp onto: a decree! He can decree that I must put aside my visions. He can demand that I take my place as one of the ordinary women of the tribe. He will try to force me to join with one of the young men. But not Varno, the Leader's son. A Leader's son may be Leader himself one day. The Old One will not give me the possibility of any place of power within the tribe.

And if I will not accept a joining? Then he will cast me out of the Golden Fish tribe in hopes that I may die before I ever reach my birth father. The Old One will do anything to save himself.

Let The Old One think for a while longer. I will simply tell the tribe who I am. Do they know what a Three Face is?

I sink into my own mind to find the future that I will describe to the people of the tribe. They are all in the compound now, sitting quietly and waiting for the judging tribunal to begin.

I will explain to them that my life will be dedicated to helping our tribe. I can call to the Spirits to bring warm seasons and abundance of food. I can coax healing from plants so our young and old can be fruitful and strong. I can lead rites for the young women to reveal their powers and teach them skills to benefit their families. I can call game into our territory, bring up fish from the sea, and discover new land for the tribe to claim as their own. Ours can become the most powerful tribe on the coast of the Great Water. There is so much I can do as a Three Face, if the Old One will allow it.

I am jarred into the present as The Old One addresses me. Even though he has called me disrespectful a few moments ago I cannot make him right about that, or anything else. The people must see me as a valid member of our tribe. If The Old One plans to cast me out he will do it, but I will make him look like the gurgling, dank old stick that he is.

Taking two steps toward The Old One I feel a thickness to the air. He has placed a protection between us. I am flattered.

"Old One, I thank you for allowing me to describe my vision quest. I know you do not have to listen to me. It is important to me that the tribe knows what I saw during the Girls' Coming of Age Rite because it is very different from what other girls saw."

The Old One answers with a sarcastic tone. "Yes, we know you are different. We know you have done many things that most girls could not do. We honor your service to Gaia and the tribe. We acknowledge you have hunted and foraged for food when your father Ruano was taken by Spirit during the hunt. Because of your efforts, you and your mother Orana have not been a burden to the tribe. But these things do not make you better than other girls who are doing what they were born to do. You seem to think you are above being an ordinary, decent woman of our tribe. But being different is not necessarily valuable. Think about what I am saying to you child, and then speak so that we may understand who you want to be."

I see what he is doing – giving me an out. He is manipulating me to feel that perhaps my visions are not important after all. If I follow his intentions, I will become just another mate and mother. Those are good things only if they are your true path.

"Old One, Savvo, Mother, you know what my vision quest showed to me. The people of our tribe do not, so it is to them I will speak." The Old One appears shaken as I turn away from him to face the people sitting quietly around the center of the compound. He deflates by several inches as I address the tribe.

"People of the Golden Fish, I am Astara, daughter of Orana and Ruano. You have watched me grow from a baby to the young woman you see before you. You know of my deeds and you know of my loneliness. Some of you are my friends and know me well – mostly the boys of the tribe. To the girls I am a wild person who talks to animals and climbs trees and swims between the waves of the Great Water at high tide to catch the golden fish in her hands.

"After the Girls' Coming of Age Rite I did not come home with the rest of the girls because my vision quest frightened me. I did not see myself in a joining ceremony, or see how many children I will bear and whether they will be girls or boys.

"I did not see a mate at all. My visions were of unknown people and places. I saw myself dressed in the gold robes of a Holy Person, mixing healing potions for the sick and communing with Spirit. Sometimes I ran in the forest as a wolf, other times I was a stag chased by a wolf. I saw myself as man and woman at the same time. I am a Three Face. The Old One himself taught us about the Three Face in Learning Circle, so we all know it is real."

The people of the tribe are murmuring now, turning quietly to one another and gesturing. Some point to me and smile, others look at me in fear, a few are laughing.

Where is Mother? She is looking proudly at me while tears drip off her cheeks and fall to the dusty ground. Savvo looks pleased in spite of his stern hawk-like profile and stoic expression.

The tribe quiets as they wait to see who will speak next. I see Varno among the crowd, smiling broadly at me as usual. He already knows who I am. There has been truth in my life all along. That is all I care about.

"I am finished speaking about my visions, Old One. I did not see myself mated or joined or with child. If the other girls saw themselves so, and the tribe honors their visions, why are my visions not honored as well? Is the Coming of Age Rite not valid for all of us? Is it fair to deny my destiny because it does not make you comfortable? The other girls' visions are honored and welcomed by the tribe. Mine showed me as man, woman and animal, a healer and seer, able to bring the best of all three into the lives of everyone. If that is what I saw on my quest, then let it be so in my life. There is no turning away from it."

The people react, murmuring and gesturing while many heads nod up and down. Some of the girls are staring at me with contempt or laughing at me, but most seem relieved by my speech. Some consider me to be one of the tribe's beauties. At least now I will not be competition for them when they try to attract a mate.

There is a disturbance in the air around me; it is The Old One. His mind hangs over an edge, grasping for the next stone. Will he throw it, or grab on for dear life? The tide of the tribe appears to be flowing my way. He desperately searches his mind for the next ploy to turn that tide against me.

Mother and Savvo look happy and supportive. The Old One's mouth is tight, ready to pronounce his next attack.

"Astara, you say you had these visions at the rite. But then you ran away. Why did you not tell the Grandmothers what you had seen? If you believed your visions were valid why not come back to the tribe and let us know what you saw? Instead you ran into the forest, exposing yourself to hostile tribes and the danger of wild animals. You returned under cloak of night like a thief – or a liar.

"I for one do not believe you saw such visions as you describe. I believe you *expected* to see them because of your eyes, because your Mother claims she was impregnated during a Spring Dreaming Ritual by a young acolyte, Thanillo, who has gone on to become Holy One of the Great Cliff tribe. It is a grandiose story your Mother probably made up to cover some shameful act that took place during the rite. Perhaps your real father was not Thanillo at all, but a man already joined with another. Why else would she have been cast out of the Great Cliff tribe to come wandering into our lands?"

Mother cuts him off like he is a young shoot destined to be chewed up for the morning meal. Her voice has a ring to it that I have not heard before.

"Old One, you speak out of turn. You know I spoke truthfully about Thanillo being Astara's birth father. You have been waiting to discredit my daughter because you already know she is a Three Face. You have seen it. There is no other explanation for your hatred of her. Until yesterday she did not know the story behind her birth. She believed Ruano was her only father. She is not putting on a show because of the story of my life. I believe you are afraid that Astara will someday push you aside as a Spirit Leader of our tribe."

The people of the tribe are stunned and speechless from Mother's words and passion. She stops herself from saying anything more. For the moment at least, her fear of The Old One is replaced by the pride she feels in me and my heritage, and in her own life. I swell toward her, capturing her words and her face in my soul.

"Orana," The Old One begins, breathing heavily and speaking carefully, "I am sorry that I questioned your premise for coming into our tribe. Yes, I saw Astara's eyes. I *do* believe what you told us about the Spring Ritual and her real father. But

I cannot think that you want this future for your only child. Do you know what being a Three Face means? Your daughter will never lead a normal life. It means she is not even human, she is man, woman, animal, and Spirit talker. Her path can never be understood by you. The way of Spirit is not easy. There is much study, many vision quests, dreams, and hard choices to make. Astara must develop wisdom in order to use her talents wisely. Thus far she has not shown much wisdom. Her action of running away from the rite shows that she lacks judgment. She will never have children; you will never have grandchildren. Your bloodline will stop with her. Is this the future you want for you and your child?"

Mother does not know what to say to this. I know she thought all these things the first night I came back home, while she lay pretending to be asleep in the dark. She does not want me to be a Three Face. But if that is what I am, I know she will stand with me. That is what a mother will do for her child, even if it hurts.

By now the tribe is talking loudly. Some people have stood up and are moving to the shade as the afternoon sun grows hot and its rays sizzle on their skin. When can this tribunal be over? I am starting to feel faint after hours in the sun, but I do not dare move to another spot. As long as we are going against each other I will stand my ground.

The Old One clears his throat. "Before I pronounce my decree regarding the girl Astara, does anyone from the tribe wish to speak?"

A murmuring rises from the people. Savvo clears his throat, and speaks before anyone else can start.

"I am Savvo, Leader of the Golden Fish tribe. I have known Astara since she was born, and I knew Orana when she first joined with my friend Ruano. She told the truth about being with child, and Astara is telling the truth about her vision quest."

A din of voices rises from the people, some agreeing and some disagreeing with Savvo.

Then Varno stands up and walks a few paces away from the crowd.

"Hello," he says with a smile, and waits for the voices to stop and for proper attention to be paid. Then with a shake of his glossy black hair, he begins.

"All of you know me. I am Varno, Savvo's last-born son." One or two of the girls make yipping noises of approval; he is considered very handsome. He goes on, "I want to speak for Astara. Most of you know that she and I are best friends. She is not lying about her vision quest because she does not know how to lie. She saw whatever it is she says she saw. I know Astara better than anyone else, and I believe she is a Three Face because she says so. She has always been able to communicate with animals. She tamed the wildcat cub, Chakka. No one else would even think of doing something like that. She talks to the deer and the squirrels. She saw her future, and I believe the tribe should accept that fact without question the same way they accept the visions of the other girls. One day I may be a Leader of the Golden Fish tribe. I am ready to accept Astara as the tribe Three Face if that is her destiny." He dips his head and backs away from the middle of the compound to sit once more on the trampled ground.

There are a few more yips, and then silence. "Does anyone else wish to speak?" the gnarled holy man invites. I am waiting to see who will stand against me. There must be someone who does not want me to be a Three Face besides The Old One.

K'Uvada rises to her feet and walks to the center of the compound. She is an older woman, the widow of one of the hunters who passed long ago. Her dark hair is streaked with white. She is tall for a member of our tribe. I wonder as I watch her move if she was born to our tribe or if she came from another tribe. She looks different, she moves different, her facial structure is different. Come to think of it, I wonder if I look different from everyone else here. All I have ever seen of myself are some wavy reflections by the water's edge.

"I am K'Uvada," she begins a bit loudly so she can be heard. The people stop talking and all eyes move to her. It is unusual for a woman to take the initiative to speak.

"I came to the Great Water tribe when I was young. I was born to the Deep Forest tribe. The hunter Doranto brought me here after I approached him in the forest. I had seen your hunters many times, so when they came near our territory during one of their hunts I hid in the bushes hoping to make contact. Doranto stepped away from the group of men and I revealed myself to him. I begged him to take me back to his tribe so I would have a chance at a new life. I am speaking because I know what it means to be a woman who wants to live her own life. The Deep Forest tribe are savages. Women are not honored there. I wanted a different kind of life for myself, so I took a chance and ran away, hoping that a man from your tribe would find me. He could have killed me, but instead Doranto was kind and brought me home with him. I was accepted by the Leader of the Great Water Tribe at that time, Savvo's father Sunno. I am in favor of letting Astara follow her visions as a member of this tribe. She has done nothing wrong. Her visions should be honored even if they do not match what others want them to be."

K'Uvada bows her head quickly and steps back to become one with the crowd. Many people clap their hands in approval of her message. I would do the same but I am glued to my spot facing The Old One, and must concentrate on keeping a straight face through this whole ordeal. I speak silently from my heart to K'Uvada as she blends into the crowd, thanking her for her courage.

The Old One stands tall and straight, waiting for others to speak. No one else comes forward. Everyone is holding their breath. The wind teases at the ends of my braid, so neatly plaited for this occasion. My good shift is saturated with sweat and the midday sun burns into my thick dark hair and turns my arms red. I am very thirsty but I have been thirsty before and I will be thirsty again. I think, *keep standing tall before this dried up Old One. His fear will make him weak.*

The Old One clears his throat and shifts his weight from one foot to the other. His tall body sways and the cowrie shells sway with it, making a pleasant sound as they tap against each other while still screening his eyes from view. I want so much to look in The Old One's eyes and see what is there. Their shape. Their color. Why are his eyes always covered, even when I confronted him in his tent?

But now he speaks and there is no more time to wonder about his eyes or anything else.

"People of the Golden Fish tribe, we have heard several people speak today concerning the girl Astara, and whether the visions she claims to have seen should be acknowledged and her chosen path honored. Or whether her visions are illusions and misdirections placed upon her by the Spirits for reasons unknown, at a vulnerable time in her life." The Old One clears his throat once more. His lies must be choking him. "Now I will speak my decree for the girl Astara."

The wind dies down and the sun moves to an angle in the sky that casts The Old One's face in a harsh glare. Some shield their eyes with their hands as they keep their eyes on The Old One. He opens his mouth to speak and I hold my breath. This is it: the decree.

"The visions the girl Astara experienced during the Girls' Coming of Age Rite cannot be incorporated into the daily life of the Golden Fish tribe. I cannot see whether they are real, or whether a malevolent Spirit has placed them on her for reasons we cannot understand. The fact that she ran away from the rite rather than speaking to the Grandmothers about her visions casts doubt on their validity, in my view."

Many voices begin speaking at once, some agreeing and some arguing this is not fair. "Silence!" says The Old One, in his normal tone that sounds like it comes from inside a rock. The people become silent.

"It is my belief the girl Astara has been led astray. This is not her fault. If she will forget her vision quest and agree to live a normal life within the tribe, all will be as it was. Astara can be joined, she can learn skills appropriate for her station as a mate and mother, she can bear children. In short, she can become a valid member of the tribe with nothing against her.

"If she insists that she must live as a Three Face, she will leave the Golden Fish tribe and make her own way as the Spirits lead her. She may go with followers or alone, it is of no concern to me, as long as she agrees to leave our tribe and *not return*. I have spoken."

The last words are lost in a clamor of voices. Some cheer and some shout at those who cheer. The tribe is divided between those who agree, and those who do not. So many are behind me!

But the decree is clear. I am given a choice. The Old One has not banished me outright, but he knows the choice I will make. He will be rid of me finally! And I will go forth on my own, waiting for Spirit to guide me. I must find a teacher. And the only teacher I want to find is my own father. I know he is Holy One of the Great Cliff tribe. I do not know how he will react when I find him, but I have to try. I want to look in his eyes. I want to see if he knows his own daughter.

Meanwhile Mother is speaking, pleading, with The Old One. "Please, Old One, Astara is a young girl. She cannot travel alone in strange and hostile lands, looking for another tribe or a cave or whatever there is to find. I remember how frightened I was when I left my home to find another tribe. I was older than Astara is now, and still I was not able to find enough food. If Ruano had not found me when he did, I would probably have starved to death or been eaten alive by wolves."

"Do not worry Orana," a voice calls out from the crowd. It is Varno. "I will travel with Astara. Who else wants to travel with Astara if she leaves our tribe?" Several other voices call out, mostly the young men who have been my playmates during my young life. I will not be alone.

"Wait!" shouts The Old One. His head swings from side to side, taking in all the people. "I have made my decree. It gives the girl Astara a choice for living the rest of her life. She must now declare her decision. It is up to her to decide her own fate. I have been generous. I do not want to see the girl suffer. It is in her hands now. She alone will decide her own fate."

A huge sound comes from the people in the compound as they excitedly repeat The Old One's words. His decree is the first of its kind. Astara is being given a choice! Which fate will she choose?

I look over at Mother. Her head is down and she tries not to show her anguish. We have already discussed my choice. Now she has a choice to make. I feel heavy and sick in my stomach because I know what her choice will be.

Savvo remains standing in his spot. In his dignity as Leader he has not moved all these hours. He has known all along what The Old One will decree. He knows his son will travel with me if I leave. He is prepared to show no feeling when I make my choice and Varno makes his.

Slowly the people comprehend I must speak my choice now, and a hush comes once more to the compound. The sun is dipping lower in the sky and the heat of the day releases, bringing the blessing of a cool breeze to the compound. My wet skin and sweaty shift feel nearly cold as the air stirs. Or I am cold inside because of the words I must speak.

"People of the Golden Fish tribe, I have lived among you for eleven seasons, soon to be twelve. You have all heard The Old One's decree.

"Here is my answer: I cannot live as an ordinary woman. I will die first. I must strike out on my own and find a tribe to accept and embrace me as a Three Face. I will seek my birth father and even if I cannot find him, I may find a tribe who has lost their own Holy One. Or a tribe who is looking for a new young leader with ideas and courage. One way or another I will find my birth father or a new tribe, or die trying. Those who wish may come with me. Most of all, I pray my mother will come with me to make my journey easier to bear."

The people seem stunned. I wait as the silence of the tribe goes on. And then a voice. "You can start your own tribe, Astara."

It is Varno. "I will come with you when you leave to make sure you are safe. We will travel together, find new people, learn new things. Any who wants to come is welcome to join us."

"Thank you, my lifelong friend. Before the decree is complete, I have one last question for The Old One." I know this is my voice but I cannot believe I have something to ask The Old One. Where is this coming from? The Old One does not seem to be able to believe it either because his head swings abruptly and there is a frown on his dark-lipped mouth.

"What question is that, Astara?" he speaks my name directly to me for the first time. I have caught him totally off guard.

"Although in my vision I am a Three Face, I know I cannot make up rites and herbal medicine and all the lore and learnings that are part of becoming a Spirit Leader. I will need a teacher. I am a clever student and in spite of what you think, I want to learn. Why can I not remain here, in the Golden Fish tribe, and learn from you? You have no acolytes. Do you not want to teach others the way of Spirit?"

I am shocked at what is coming from my mouth! I do not want to learn from The Old One! I am not sure what is making me speak these words; all I know is that my heart wants to know the answer to this question. There is more to The Old One's animosity for me than anyone suspects. There is something yet to be revealed.

The Old One was not expecting this question any more than I was expecting to ask it. The cowrie shells swing as his head shakes slightly from side to side, and his dark fingers move restlessly on his staff.

He breathes in deeply before he speaks. "Why do you ask this of me? Why do you want me to teach you now when you never wanted to learn from me before? You throw your words at me like dung!" His voice is like stones grinding together in the surf, his mouth speaking the words without control, his teeth nearly wagging back and forth in mounting fury.

I do not care if he is angry. My mother is in pain.

"I do not want to leave this tribe, Old One. I am trying to think of a way I can stay with my mother and still follow my path." I speak simply, without knowing what I am going to say, but when the words leave my mouth I know they are true.

The heads of the whole tribe move as one back and forth between me and The Old One, caught up in our exchange. As people absorb the fact I am leaving and Orana is staying behind the murmurs begin again. What will become of her? She cannot hunt for herself and she is too old to join with a new mate. How will she live without me?

"Do not worry about your mother, Astara. I will make sure she has enough food. She can live with my family if she is lonely. Since Varno will be gone we will have an open spot at our fire."

It is Savvo speaking. "Orana, you and I will talk about our children over the night embers, all the while knowing they are safe because they are together."

The hush of the afternoon, the waft of a rising breeze, and the rhythm of high tide hypnotize everyone. The Old One is looking straight at Savvo now. I can feel heat coming from the invisible eyes. He is angry at Savvo, but tribal law says a Leader cannot be challenged when he offers his hearth to a member of the tribe.

"This is unexpected Savvo, and very kind. I will think about what I must do," says Mother. She tilts her face toward the heavens and her mouth moves. I know she talks to the Spirits, asking them for guidance.

"Thank you, Savvo," I say. I bow down to the ground in homage. He will help my mother. I will leave the Golden Fish tribe with Varno, and together we will travel the cliff side trail to the land of the Great Cliff tribe, to find my birth father and my fate.

Mother and I do not speak as we walk back to her tent. There is not much to say. I know she will not come with me. I wish she would, but she will stay here with the tribe that took her in so long ago. And I will leave.

"Astara," Mother says. I wait to hear what she wants to tell me but she says nothing more. I feel her head turn toward me as we near her tent.

"I am listening."

"I want you to go. I will miss you, but you need to follow your destiny as I followed mine. Do not worry about me. I will be fine. Savvo is kind. I belong here."

"Why not come with me? I do not want to leave without you! What will happen when you are older and I am not here to care for you? That should also be my destiny. What kind of daughter am I?"

"You will be a Spirit leader by that time, and you will always be my daughter. I pray you can return to our tribe to take care of me. I will look for you every day." We reach our tent and she does not look at me or wait for an answer, but lifts the flap and goes inside.

I stay outside for a while memorizing the sights of our part of the tribal compound. The hard bark of an oak tree contrasts with the shaggy russet bark of a cedar. The shrubbery is thick behind the tent. I cannot follow her in yet. I do not know what to say to her, or how long I will be gone. I should gather my things and get some sleep, but instead I sit down on the ground to think.

I will take a thick sleeping hide made of otter skin; the fur on the inside is short, warm and silky, not too bulky for traveling. A few shifts can be rolled in with it. For grooming I will bring a dried teasle for my hair, and one ash and lard patty. The water will always be on our left, so I will always be clean. Should I not have an amulet in which to carry a relic from our tribe? A Three Face should carry a token of some significance. I start looking on the ground for an unusual stone or a shell. No, an amulet should have meaning. There is no time to prepare.

"Are you coming inside?" I start at Mother's voice.

"I am thinking."

"All right, dear. I will wrap some food for your journey in the meantime."

Always thinking of me. And all I can think of is myself and what I am going to do. Whether I am a he, she or an it. The Old One is right about me, never thinking about anyone else, selfish and disrespectful.

"Do not worry about what The Old One says about you. He is jealous." Mother's voice is muffled through by the thick hide of our tent. She always reads my mind.

I duck my head inside and we spend our last night together, eating and preparing for my journey. We laugh together as if tonight is any other night, but behind our smiles is a chasm of loneliness and uncertainty. Life is about to change and thinking about it is exhausting.

I put my head down on my sleeping furs and in no time, I am floating on the wings of a new and strange dream.

Floating higher above the horizon than I have ever been. Is this sleep? A warm smell of rich tea soothes me.

This is all about love. Life as a Three Face is probably important and will be exciting but it will also be lonely. I cannot hide here far above the world pretending that I do not hurt. Where is everyone I love?

Where is Mother? I try to see through heavy sea mist but our tent is obscured. I hear the Great Water surging below but it is invisible. I love the people in my life. My mother. Ruano, father of my heart. Varno, even Savvo, and everyone in our Golden Fish tribe that took Mother in and sustained my life. But after I leave these people will fade. I will not be living with them, they will not be my family; even Mother will become a stranger. Varno will be my companion and friend, but we will not join. My life will be full of experiences but empty of love. There will be learning, new tribes, Spirit ceremonies and new robes decorated with beadwork depicting my deeds and visions, but these are not love.

Will Thanillo know me and love me as his daughter when he sees my eyes? I know nothing about my eyes except what everyone tells me about them. They are Thanillo's eyes. When I see him, will I finally recognize a missing piece of myself?

Too late. I have left Gaia and I am in an unknown place. Questions that I have never asked are in my mind with no one alive to answer them.

Who do I *really* love? Who would I walk out onto the edge of a cliff for? I do not know the answer, do not ask me this, I do not want to know.

Of course I know. I have always known.

Before there was knowing there were secrets of the heart, loving others, loving the self. Only in living did I forget about love. But it is all right. There is no one to please here. The trees are not standing in judgement of me. They do not even know I am here. I am inconsequential. There is no one to disappoint. Honesty is not a liability here.

Whose voice is this? I remember this voice. Is it something I will hear many times when I sit dreaming in a cave, cross-legged and eyes staring into the fire, hearing only the sounds of the sea crashing endlessly in the dark?

There will be darkness for a long while. My mind is the blank I will try to reach throughout my whole life as a Three Face, but will never succeed in finding. Perhaps this is the place of knowing, where I was meant to go; a place in the future where I try to take my tribe, a place that eludes me.

I remember a life by the Great Water. That life was filled with sadness and loss, but also with learning and friendship. I felt full and complete.

And then there was another life.

Do not be afraid. You are a Three Face.

I fall through the green mist and settle downward. I lie quietly where I fall, a leaf on the ground. I smell the familiar scents of pine and moss. Something is coming to me that I have never seen before.

A woman. The life of a woman in a vast place of roaring noise and rafts that move without water. A word comes to me; cars. And bigger rafts, called trucks. And even bigger ones that fly like birds.

A smell like a tea but richer, thick and nurturing in the morning. A friend with hair the color of flames, and a little child whom I love. A man with dark hair, laughter, comfort. Living in a strange cave with openings covered in something clear like sea water, only hard, letting light stream in. And cats! Is Chakka here? I fall and cannot move but feel no fear. The floor of this cave is not earth, but made of hard flat stones.

I am carried in one of those trucks engulfed in blaring noise and light. People wearing white Spirit skins sit near or move around me. Other skins the color of sky stretch over their noses and mouths leaving only their eyes showing. Strange. The Old One covers his eyes and these Spirit people show theirs. More people than I have ever seen, with brown eyes like my tribe, or bright blue eyes of all things, and people with very dark skin! The Spirit people lift me onto a flat slab raised up from the ground, moving swiftly by means of small round stones – wheels – amid jarring noises, loud voices, bouncing from the truck into a large cave. People all in white. They must be Holy Ones.

This is not a place in my imagination. It is real. This is my real life in another place and time.

This dream is of my life as Evelyn. Evie. A woman in the future.

CHAPTER EIGHT

I am Evie. I thought I was Astara. Evie and Astara. I am two people, but the same person. How can that be?

I am awake.

I'm not in the forest anymore, rotting with the dark leaves and green moss. There is no thrush here. There *is* the sound of heavy surf. Sea spray rains down on my head even though the surf sounds like it is a distance below.

I've been sleeping to one side of a stony path trailing along the edge of a cliff. I look up and out over a vast expanse of unbelievably blue water. My neck is killing me, and my knees and right pinky are stiff. I crawl to the edge of the cliff so I can look down without worrying about going over. I stick my head out over the edge as a huge wave crashes against the cliff, shooting water up to soak my face and hair and falling back in hissing foam over massive rock formations that slice darkly out of the sea. The boom of surf is hypnotic and sounds further away than it is. The sea smells clean as it courses down my face, refreshes for a second, then evaporates in the intense sunlight beating down on my head. I reach up without thinking and push my wet hair behind my ears. What happened? It's so short!

Another wave rolls in and thunders against the cliff; I withdraw my head in time to avoid a dousing.

Sea gulls call from above, fighting over a piece of crab. They swoop next to my face and I get a good look. They appear to be Herring gulls, but with some slight difference; it's their eyes. I recall that Herring Gulls have yellow eyes, but these are oxblood red. The birds fly so near I can see sunlight shining through the breathing holes in their heavy beaks. At least I still remember something about birds.

Now I'm Evie again.

I feel like Evie; stiff back, stiff knees, and my neck? Well, I don't want to think about my neck. Odds are there are no pain pills here.

Is this for real? Jumping back and forth between lives? I scratch my head and pull the hair forward for a better look. Chin length and thick, dyed golden brown now to mimic the former natural color. How long have I been sleeping here? Days. Years. My roots must be starting to show.

I recall setting out with at least one companion, but nobody is here. It would be best to get away from the edge of this cliff, so I crawl back to the rutted path. The sun feels like it is eating away at the thin skin over my breastbone. I've learned something from being Astara: it is midday. Where in the world am I?

I stand up too quickly and my head whirls. I sneak a look at my hands but already know what I'll see – Evie's hands with short, strong nails, no polish, the fingers knobbed with slightly swollen knuckles from digging in my garden, playing guitar, scrubbing the bathtub, the arthritic right pinky joint swollen red. The skin is dry with prominent blue veins.

I miss Astara's hands.

"Varno! *Vaaarnooo!*" I shout into the wind. If he is here, which I doubt, he'll never hear me yelling. The surf is too loud.

I've never been here in Evie's lifetime, but the place is totally familiar. This is a landscape from Astara's life. I don't feel hunger or thirst, but I'd at least like to know for sure which life I'm in right now.

I review what I know. I came to this place, wherever it is, took the form of nothing more than a thought process, then woke up in a new body, time and place as Astara. I experienced several days as a young girl living in the Mesolithic era, and now I'm here alone in her world as me. That is, Evie.

Since I hit the floor in my 21st Century kitchen there has been one constant. I don't understand anything.

A prayer from Evie's life. Please. God, Jesus, Buddha, Mohammad, Guardians, Galaxies, Universe, forces, stars, suns, moons, spirits seen and unseen. Please. Help me.

Is it urgent? It's peaceful, the sun is warm, and I don't need anything right now except to know what's happened to me. Oh, and some fresh water and food would be nice.

So, nothing urgent. Having asked for help, I sit down to wait on the side of the path under a tree, enjoying the shade after the bracing surf facial and blinding sun.

I would love to see a friendly face. Who in my life was always there to lift me, never judged me, always made me feel like I knew what I was doing? Was there ever anyone like that?

Whoever that is, that's who I'd like to find now. The surf endlessly crashing against the cliff sends cool droplets of sea mist up to the path. The wind is light, the shade is relaxing and I close my eyes. The next time I open them I want to be somewhere else where there is a person to encourage and help me.

❧❦

I must have dozed off. Do I remember wishing to be in another place?

Let's do it over. Close my eyes, listen, breathe in the scents of – nothing. Open my eyes. I am surrounded by white space, no sound, no path, no cliff. Nothing to feel. Nothing to hear. I close and open my eyes again, expecting – what? I am still here in white space with nothing.

What do I know about white space? From art and literature, I know that white space defines and brings attention to a word, an image, a thing. If that is correct I am sure to be found here, since there is a lot of white space around me.

It is odd, but soothing. I'm not in control. This landscape is a respite from worry and care. No smells, no needs, no dirt, no shadows, just white.

Still, I want to be found. I shout, "Anybody here?" The sound of my voice falls against me like a slight shove. It's just me and white space.

I sit down. No sense standing. If anyone else comes along they are sure to see me. What nonsense I'm thinking. This place forces you to become stupid. Or calm. I have finally slowed down to where I can think and decide, instead of always reacting and running to the next thing. My life as Astara was a lot of reaction to things beyond my control. Urgent needs had to be met simply to remain alive. Finding food, water, and shelter. Learning how to live in a hostile world. Avoiding people who could kill me. My life as Evie was more in control, wasn't it? Or was it also a series of reactions to acquire the essentials of life, elicit responses from people, and call it living? At least when I was Evie I wasn't in immediate danger of being killed, or of starving.

I hear something. Clop tap. Clop tap. Clop tap. I speak out loud for something to do.

"What is that, a horse? I would love to see a horse out here."

My words are swallowed quickly by the vacuum.

I squint into the distance and see nothing. Clop tap, clop tap, clop tap. The regular sound of someone in leather-soled shoes walking toward me, not fast or slow, far off, without urgency, but definitely coming toward me.

After staring for a long time, I determine that the sound is accompanied by a blur, or my eyes may simply be tired. Is the blur getting darker, the clopping and tapping marginally louder? How far away is the blur? Could it speed up please? This might take hours or days. I'm forced to admit I've got time.

Am I imagining things, or is the blur darker with a vaguely human shape? I'm certain the blur has a defined top and two lower protrusions. Legs? Are they moving in time to the clop tap? I'm going to say yes, and yes to the question of whether there are vestigial arms.

The blur becomes more solid. I rise to my feet to watch clop tap interminably coming toward me. Lara? It has a vague shape of a head and smudges that might be a face, and the top of the head is flat with a sheen like grey metal. It isn't Lara; her hair is auburn red and long. Besides, what would she be doing here with dead people?

The blur takes on the color of a Gulf Stream blue shirt with splashes of yellow. The body looks male, the legs are tan and bare to the knees, wearing off-white shorts. The smudge face is smiling, the grey metal hair is cut in military style with shaved sides and flat top. The eyes are dark glasses, so no eyes yet. Like The Old One except this presence is friendly, even loving.

How do I know that? The white space is bringing the love into focus. It's a strange feeling.

The blur has become a man. What am I wearing? I don't have to look to know. It's my everyday uniform. I have to thank whoever dressed me: favorite V-neck T-shirt of faded black embossed with Chinese characters and colorful birds, comfortable shorts of stone-washed coral pink cotton. All the clothes are clean, which is a switch from what I've been used to recently, and I can feel that I'm wearing underwear. I'm also wearing my favorite white leather sneakers, presumably so I can get away fast if I don't like what I see. Not that there's anywhere to go.

Clop tap is closing in on me and I'm able to see more, but I still don't know who it is. It's not Paul; even if he has aged he would never have a military haircut. Oh, why can't it be Paul? I don't know another man I want to see or talk to. There's no one else I can trust or, if I'm qualified to say the word, love.

I try speaking, even though the last attempt was a failure. "Hello", I say. The words don't fall against me this time, they seem to move out toward the man. They sound flat, without feeling.

"I thought you would be happy to see me." The voice is warm and tinged with humor. I look intently at the face, the smiling mouth. I think I know the face. I haven't seen it in a long time so I can't be sure.

"Take off your glasses," I say, but it sounds so impersonal, so I add, "please."

"Evie, you can do better than that! Don't you know me? Remember the clove hitch?" asks the man with an encouraging smile.

Clove hitch? What the hell does that mean?

Then it hits me. The clove hitch is a sailor's knot. I remember standing on the deck of a sailboat and someone I know well showing me how to tie a clove hitch. "Funny name for a knot," he says, rubbing the stubble on his chin in thought. "I have no idea why they call it a clove hitch."

"Well," I say in my librarian voice, "it's because there are two loops that split the knot in half, in other words, cloven in two. So, a clove hitch." I smile up at the man.

"My, my Evie," the man says, "I never realized that, but you're absolutely right! You are a lexicon of information!" I felt so happy in that novel moment of validation. I remember that afternoon so clearly. Why can't I remember the man?

"Relax. I'm here to help. Even though you have spent your life rejecting all help as I recall." The voice still sounds like a smile. One beefy hand, dotted with liver spots, reaches up to swipe off the sunglasses. "Better now?" clop tap man asks.

Uncle Larrson! What's he doing here?

"It's you!" I'm finally sure now, as the blur that became a man stands a few feet away. His eyes are a clear, light blue and he is still smiling.

How long has it been? When did he die? I was so sad when I lost Uncle Larrson. He was the only adult man in my life who ever gave me encouragement. My Dad never did; like The Old One, he was focused on my shortcomings, perhaps trying to teach me the hard way. Uncle Larrson was the only one who seemed proud of me when I graduated high school and then college, went out on my own and got a good job and then a great raise, all on my own merit. The clove hitch. I remember now.

Without thinking I walk five steps and we're standing face to face. "Hi Evie, it's such a treat to see you. Getting older is not as much fun as we thought it would be, is it?" He opens his arms to me and we hug a warm and relaxing hug I've needed for ages.

I'm filled with emotion and confusion. Tears sting my eyes but I'm not sad. "Thank you for coming to me!" I'm babbling now, holding him at arm's length and looking up into those impish, accepting eyes. "I've needed to talk to someone who knows what's going on. I'm glad you're here. I know you can help me. Where is this? Is this even a place? A lot of strange stuff has happened to me since that day in the kitchen," I trail off.

"Relax now. I'll explain everything. A lot of people don't understand but I know you will. You've always been one of the smartest people I know."

"You always made me feel like I was smart when no one else did." I remember that much about my life, but not much more. I'm already a different person.

Someone is missing. "Where's Aunt Toni?" I blurt out. "I miss her so much! I know she could explain a lot of things to me too. Isn't she here with you?

"She certainly is. Antonia is off visiting with some of the others. After I left all of you, she and I stayed in touch for all those years. She knew we would be together again. Do you remember her diary, the one you and Theodora found in her apartment?"

How could I forget? We found Aunt Antonia's journal when we went through her apartment after she passed. She wrote about all the times she had experienced Uncle Larrson answering her thoughts through lights flashing up from the water in the canal outside their house in South Carolina, or in a snatch of his voice carried on the morning breeze. "Theo thought Aunt Toni had lost her mind," I said, "but I knew she was talking to you. Why worry about whether she was or not anyway? It was real for her, so it didn't matter whether we believed it or not."

Larrson and Toni had shared the same goals in life. Build a sailboat, live on the water, and sail up and down the East Coast and out to the Bahamas whenever they wanted. For years they never spent any money to the point of living in a permanently half-finished fixer-upper, and Larrson was retired by age 45. They built the boat, even choosing and chopping down the pine tree for the main mast, and moved to South Carolina so they could live on the water before they got all dried up and life ebbed away from them. The sloop was real enough, quietly rocking in the canal outside their back porch, always ready for another adventure into the Gulf Stream or an overnight jaunt to one of the marinas down by Hilton Head.

They knew what they were doing. That's what I need, to speak to someone who knows what they're doing. God knows, I never did.

I'm afraid to change the subject, but since coming here there have been so many questions! Now I can barely remember any of them, but I have one to ask now. "Uncle Larrson, I need to know something. Where the hell am I?"

He laughs out loud at that, his smile making me relax again, the icy blue eyes squinting in that knowing way he has. "You're in an in-between place where you can find out things you need to know in order to move on to the next stage of your life."

"What do you mean, my life? I'm dead. Didn't anyone tell you?" I'm surprised he doesn't know.

"Let's forget about that for a while. Tell me who you think I am."

"I already did. You're Uncle Larrson. You look like him anyway. Are you real?" I'm getting confused again.

"I'm as real as I can be. Don't you know I never left you? Can you remember anything from before?" He looks at me like this is a test and I need to come up with the right answer or be stupid forever.

I can see the words in Times New Roman sitting on the air so they're easy to review. I repeat them, hoping that understanding will come to me soon. "I've never left you. Meaning, "you've never left me" I guess."

"Go on," he says indulgently, "you're on the right track."

"You've never left me. You've been with me." I think hard about this. How could he be with me after he died, or even when he was still alive in South Carolina? Did I feel him always watching out for me? Maybe. Wait. Is he one of the nameless ones I have always known were watching over me, helping me, keeping me alive and safe through near car crashes, crazy men in Mexico, getting caught under the float when the wave hit us at the beach and I nearly drowned? That's it! He's one of my Guardians.

"I heard you every time you thanked your Guardians, or prayed to us when you were scared or needed help. Most of your prayers were for Lilly, or for sick friends and family. We heard you all along and we always will. Do you know how many Guardians you have?"

Yes. Or no. "I think I know some but I have no way of knowing if I'm right about any of them."

"You do now. I'm telling you that all the Guardians you thought you had are real. And there are many more that you don't know you have, but we're all looking out for you. That's the way it works."

"I hoped. I believed. But I never knew for sure."

"I think you did. Why else did you always talk to us? Every Guardian you spoke to is real. We've all been watching you, keeping you on track, keeping you from harm. We all hear your prayers. Believe it."

"Okay, I believe it. But that doesn't answer my questions about where I am now. What is this place? Can I ever get out of here? I don't even care where I go."

"Well you did go somewhere, didn't you?" He's testing me again, and again I'm going to be stupid if I don't get it right.

"I was Astara for a while, so I guess she's me. Will I ever see her again?"

"You might. Do you want to go back and see what she does with her life? You could learn something." The way he's talking makes me think I should go back. I *am* curious to see what she – what I – did after I left the Golden Fish tribe. Funny how I can go back and forth between her memories and mine. Why didn't I know about her before?

"Why did I wake up in Astara's body after I died?"

"Why do you think you did?"

"I *think* she's the original me." Is there reassurance in his face? He smiles and puts out his hands making a "come to me" gesture with his fingers.

"She's the first time my soul took a human form and came to Earth to live, isn't she?"

"You're on to something." He still smiles, and nods his head. He's waiting for me to go on.

"You're telling me that reincarnation is a real thing? That we keep coming back as one person or thing, then another, then another, working out all the things we did wrong, paying off our bad karma." I talk fast, slapping my hands on my sides in exasperation. "We live over and over again, and don't remember a thing?"

"It's not over and over. And we're not paying off bad things with life after life. It's more subtle. Our souls wait for the right human. We live, we pass back in order to rejuvenate, and we wait for another opportunity. We choose the *right* opportunity. We choose when to finish what we started. Or to start something new."

It's a lot to digest. "So how many me's have there been?"

"Tell me what you feel."

"Why are we having a guessing game? Why can't you tell me what's going on?"

"Because that's why you are given life. To find out for yourself. There's no right and wrong except by your own measurement. We are born knowing the difference between good and evil. We are born with innate knowledge that we may bury below our surface, but it's always guiding us. We choose which path to take."

A lot to think about. My paths unfolded as though there was no choice, and all along I *was* choosing although I didn't know it, and although I didn't always choose correctly.

"You can choose now whether you want to go back to Astara's life, or whether you want to look back on Evie's lifetime."

"How do I know which is the right choice? It seems like it's important."

"It is if you want to know more about your life as Evie. Astara was your first attempt at living as a human on the Earthly plane. You did well, but there are lessons for you there if you want to take the time to find them."

I look down at my white sneakers as if they have the answer. "You're saying I should go back to see what Astara does after she leaves the Golden Fish tribe."

I look up for clues on his face, but he is not there. I am back on the path by the cliff. It is early morning, and I am watching the comic twitch of Varno's face in the throes of a dream.

CHAPTER NINE

"Varno," I whisper. I do not want to wake him but it is time we ate something and started walking. "Wake up now. Time to go." He dreams on, I take my right foot and slowly push it into his dusty leg.

"What!" he sits up quickly, feeling for his knife and looking right and left with wide dark eyes.

"It is only me! You were dreaming," I say with a smile. "We should have some tea. We have a long walk ahead of us."

He jumps to his feet gracefully, shaking out his straight, jet black hair. His slightly slanted eyes are almost as dark as his hair. "You should plait your hair like mine," I tell him as dust rises from his skin and clothes.

"You are lucky that your mother plaited your hair before we left," he says smiling back at me, "but who will plait mine? Do you know how to do stuff like that? Girl stuff?"

"I know how to make a braid at least. You do not need to be a girl to do that, all you need are fingers." Mother's braids are much tighter and finer than mine. We have been walking for many days now. I do not think Varno has noticed I have washed and plaited my hair several times since we left our tribe.

"I am ready for some tea," he says.

I have the fire going near a boulder to shield the flames from blowing out in the steady sea breeze. I brought a boiling bag made from extra thick hide and Varno has a skin for water. We use sticks to flick sizzling stones from the fire into the heating bag of water. After doing this a few times the water is bubbling and I toss some dandelion and peppermint leaves that I found this morning into the hot water. Tea will wake us up and give us energy. We have plenty of dried meat strips and pine nuts to chew as we walk.

"It cannot be much longer now. I know we always think of the other tribes as distant relatives, but we have been walking for one and a half Moons. What did your mother tell us about how we would know when we were getting near?" Varno sounds like he is wondering if the Great Cliff tribe exists. I am starting to wonder the same thing.

"Do you think something happened to all of them?" I think out loud as I stare over the cliffs into the mist that covers the horizon line beyond the Great Water.

"Like what?" Varno says absently, but his eyes narrow while he speaks.

"A sickness. Or they moved to another place. It has been a long time since Mother left them."

"What are the landmarks?"

"Mother said she remembers many more pine nut trees growing more thickly as we get near the perimeter of tribal lands. The cliff edge twists and turns at that point instead of being straight." I am trying to visualize Mother's description.

Varno does not seem to be listening. He is looking up the path.

I look in the same direction to see a man standing about one hundred paces up the cliff path. He carries a staff in his hand. Does he have a weapon? I cannot see in the morning glare. His hair appears light, as if covered in ashes. He is lean and wears a white robe and something white on his legs. I squint to see what it is – skins covering both legs individually? It is a strange garb.

Varno's legs are farther apart now and his fingers are tight on his knife. He stops moving and chewing; a mouthful of dried meat distends one cheek. Only his hair stirs in the breeze.

The man begins walking toward us at a leisurely pace, but I feel his stare penetrating my face even at this distance. Long legs cover the ground quickly and he stops about fifty paces away, near enough for me to see his eyes narrow and his brows pull down as he stares more intently at me. I can see his hair better now. It is not covered in ashes but simply light brown, reaching down to his shoulders and somewhat wavy like mine. Varno's stance has relaxed a bit. He must see as I do that the man carries no weapon, only a long staff wrapped at the top with red leather and very large white feathers from some kind of raptor. The man's robes appear to be covered in beadwork. A Holy Man?

Chakka jumps out from behind a boulder and trots up the path toward the man with her striped tail held high. The man smiles and raises his hand slightly higher than shoulder height, palm outward toward us.

Without thinking I copy his gesture, then cast a furtive glance at Varno. His eyes have gone wide.

"And what is that?" he hisses.

"A greeting. He seems friendly."

"He *seems* friendly but we do not know for sure, do we?" Varno whispers from the side of his mouth as he copies my gesture and starts walking toward the man.

Chakka sits in the middle of the path licking a front paw and smoothing it over her ears, face and whiskers. When we catch up to her she joins our procession with a purposeful step. I put my hand down to touch her damp nose. "It is alright Chakka. We will find out who he is." She shifts green eyes up to mine then pushes up with her hind legs to bump her head against my hand.

"Is that your wildcat?" the man calls out. At the sound of his voice I stop walking and look up. While I was petting Chakka I did not notice how close we had come to him.

"She is my friend. I found her when she was a cub and she decided to stay with me. The choice to stay or go is hers."

"A wise answer," he says and almost smiles. His face is kind but there are many furrows in his forehead. I try to look at Varno to gauge his feelings. "It seems you have made a choice too. Who is this with you, girl?" he continues with a calm voice.

"I am Varno," said with a touch of defiance. "We are travelers."

"I dreamed of your arrival last night," says the brown-haired man, "and have come to see the girl from my dream, with long dark hair and eyes like deep water and honey. You have traveled far." He takes a step. His eyes remain focused on my face.

"Come no closer!" says Varno evenly and with strength. "We do not know you."

"Wait Varno," I say, "there is something familiar here. And he mentioned my eyes." I think, *Why has he not told us his name?*

"Do you know Orana?" I did not know I was going to say that, and I immediately regret bringing Mother into this moment.

"What do you seek here girl?" the man says, his voice abruptly dry and without color. Why did he change so quickly?

"I ask if you know Orana," I say quietly. "I can stare at you the same way you stare at me until you answer my question." I feel Varno's face sweep sideways toward me in surprise and read his thoughts. *We do not know this man. Try to follow the rules of polite speech at least!*

"Varno, this man dreamed of me and I can tell he knows my mother. He has not asked me my name or told us his. Now he must tell us who he is."

"As you say, girl whose mother is Orana, I knew her long ago when she lived among my people, the Great Cliff tribe. She and I were friends."

I start walking slowly toward him. Chakka moves along with me. If there was danger I think she would run, so I continue walking. Varno's eyes grow larger as he keeps pace with me. We stop at five paces from the man.

"You *are* the girl I dreamed about last night," he says in amazement. "Why are you here?"

"I am Astara of the Golden Fish tribe. My Mother is Orana, who came to the Golden Fish tribe after she was cast out of the Great Cliff tribe for finding herself with child by an acolyte who became a Holy Follower of your Holy One. I am looking for that acolyte. I have walked a long way to find him." I continue to stare into the man's eyes.

"I am Thanillo," he says. His face shows nothing, and his eyes tell all. He has eyes like deep water, dark forest, and golden fire, eyes like no other except me. "I am that acolyte. I am your father."

❧

The word repeats in Evie's mind over and over. *Father, father.*

No, you're not! You're Uncle Larrson. I was asking you a question and you disappeared. You can't change and decide to be my father now. Like an echo in a vast cave the word rolls over itself in my head until the reverberation becomes unbearable. I shut my eyes and put my fingers in my ears.

I know I'm Evie again. I'm starting to get used to the changes back and forth. I hate it here in the white place when there's no one to talk to.

"Uncle Larrson!" I call out. The vacuum absorbs my voice. I sit down to wait.

It's a long time before I see a faint blur in the distance. The blur seems to have a shadow component. Having nothing better to do, I challenge myself to stare at the blur without blinking. It slowly takes on more distinct form but my eyes start to burn and I blink. Now there is a faint clopping sound like before, when I met Uncle Larrson the first time. The blur is still very far away.

Before the blur arrives I have some time to wonder at the strangeness of this place. For one thing, there is no tunnel. The people who describe near death – that's what this must be – always talk about being drawn to a tunnel of light with shadowy figures and singing angels. Many people experience overwhelming love, peace and euphoria. But I haven't seen any tunnels, there are no singing angels, and I am still looking for love. Uncle Larrson said I would learn something about myself by going back to see what happened to Astara. I learned that she found her father after walking for a while on the cliff path, but I didn't learn anything else about me. What is happening to *me*?

Why am I not hungry? Where did these clothes come from? Why am I here? What happened to me after the ambulance took me away from my home?

"You certainly have a lot of questions," says Uncle Larrson.

The sound of his voice startles me and I look up. "Don't scare me like that!"

"I've brought Aunt Toni to see you."

"Aunt Toni!" I shout and look around to his left and right. I don't see her. Then she steps out from behind him with a big smile on her face.

"Hi Evie. It's good to finally see you again." The dark brown eyes are slightly slanted up at the corners and her cheekbones are high. She has a straight nose, and her hair is a fine medium brown, perfectly straight.

"Aunt Toni!" I jump to my feet, put my arms around her and bury my face in her shoulder, smelling her familiar scent, like crushed lemons. She's about my height but much stockier.

"I've missed you so much!" I want to hug her and never stop.

"Larrson told me you were here, and I am so glad it's you," she says.

"Who else would I be?"

"Sometimes someone turns up here who isn't who you thought they'd be." She waves her hand like she's pushing something away. "This is a funny place. Lost people come here to find out who they are and what they're supposed to do with their life. But I know you'll find your own answers."

Lost people come here to find out what they're supposed to do with their life? The more I find out the more confused I am.

"Aunt Toni, I've been finding out some things about a person I used to be."

"Oh?" she says, listening now with interest.

Larrson interjects, "What she means is that she is finding out about her soul's journey."

"Oh, yes, of course." This explanation seems to clarify things for Aunt Toni.

It's clarifying something for me too. I have a soul. It's real. The first time it took on human form I was a courageous girl named Astara. Instead of being impatient and asking a lot of questions, I should be quiet and learn from what happened to her.

Larrson and Toni look at me in amusement. "Are you guys reading my mind?"

"It's not that hard, dear," says Toni, polite but with an eyebrow raised.

"Okay. Without disappearing again and leaving me in the lurch, what do you two think I should do now? Is there more to learn about my life as Evie by going back to see how Astara is doing with her life? I have to admit, her life is more interesting than mine ever was. She's quite a woman!"

Aunt Toni speaks quietly, taking my face in her hands and fixing her slanted eyes on mine. "Astara learns some life lessons I think you need to live and feel, the same way that she felt them. You lived as Evie without letting yourself feel any of your lessons. You've let your lessons numb you instead of letting them open you so your soul can finally be alive! You need to stop hiding from who you are."

She's holding onto my face so tightly I can hardly answer. "Aunt Toni, I don't want to feel my lessons," I say through my scrunched mouth. "I know who I am."

"So you say. To make sense of what you've done in your life as Evie, you need to feel the emotions that Astara felt in a time where people lived and acted without distractions."

Before I can answer, Aunt Toni blows in my face, her hands hard on my cheeks so I can't get away or speak. She lets go and I feel myself flying backward and down, holding my breath as I go into a cool envelope that covers my skin and hair in a rush, and leaves me weightless in a kind of baptism.

CHAPTER TEN

My heart is pounding a hole into my chest and throat. I cannot stay here anymore. *I have to do this! No thinking anymore. Run!*

Anyone looking out at the cliff face and near-dawn horizon would be surprised to see a female figure running with strong legs and pumping arms to leap over the cliff edge. The figure flies out over the edge for what seems like a long moment, weightless like the albatross that lives for seven years soaring over the sea, sleeping on silent air with its wing tendons locked, flying low between dark swells. But unlike the stately albatross, I am weightless for only an instant.

A wave smashing loudly into the rough cliff face reaches its tentacles upward to pull me down. Then there is the plummet toward thrashing surf, and I am shocked by how quickly I fall with no time to think. Shocked by the force of my body when it hits, with no time to feel hurt or loss. Water covers me coldly and turns me upside down, forcing sand and salt foam into my mouth. As I tumble I notice I am still holding my breath.

Breathe! Breathe it in and get it over with!

I cannot do it. I clamp down on my breath with my throat and chest and try to figure out which way is up. This is not what I prayed for.

The life force is stronger than sorrow after all. Then why did my Shanara die? I thought I wanted to die too, but all I want is to live without pain. None of my wishes will come true. I see now that my life will continue and I will feel everything. There is nothing left for me in life, but I do not know how to choose death.

Churning waves toss me against jagged boulders. The blow is softened by the fact that I am still under water, hearing the hollow bubbles bounce against stone. If I want to live I must get away from this part of the cliff and find a smoother way to shore. I am not trying to swim; I know that if I hold still Gaia and the Sky Spirits will send me to the surface so I can breathe again.

But first, another swell rolls me backward like an empty shell while sand rasps my skin raw and forces its way up my nose. Then a giant hand of water shoves me swiftly into the boulders again. I put out my arm to protect my face and immediately see a bloom of blood rise from where sharp stone cuts my palm and inner arm. The wind is knocked out of me. I could die now.

My head bobs to the surface and I gulp air with a screaming gasp. Red feathers of blood twist up from my knees and arms and sit on the surface foam for a second. I chose my spot well for dying. I need to get out of the water before I attract sharks.

The next wave is less powerful and I try to stroke sideways to get away from this killing place. I remember a crescent beach down from here, about fifty land paces away. Blood streams into my eyes and salt water pours from my nose. I run a hand over my face to clear my vision. My head must have bashed into stone at some point, but there is no pain.

The water flattens out for a moment. Here is my chance. Stroke! Stroke! I hear voices above me now. The tribe must not see me floundering here. It will not do for them to realize their Three Face has tried to end her own life.

"Astara!"

Who is calling my name? I do not care. Truly. It is of no importance. Nothing is important anymore.

As though it hears my thoughts and agrees, the ocean spits me up onto the beach, shoving my face into wet pebbles. Lapping surf drags my hair back and forth, instantly packing it with sand. I am cast out of the sea with the dead things, but I am not dead. With heavy arms and legs, I can only lie here and wait to feel the sun on my face. My burning eyes focus on blood seeping from my body into the rough sand, bleeding back and forth against me with the movement of the tide.

"Astara! What happened?" I recognize Varno's urgent voice over the sound of clattering shells and pebbles being dragged at ear level. Always Varno. When will he ever leave me alone? Everything is his fault. No, I correct myself, that is not right. Do not blame him for my mistakes.

I hear feet pumping hard on pebbles and a second later he skids to my side, knee splashing blood into my eyes. His hands scoop my face out of the water as he speaks in confusion, "How did you fall over the cliff? Were you pushed? Who did this to you?"

I am too exhausted to answer so I look deep into his eyes and send my message. His expression slackens and he looks away.

"Why?" is all he can say. *How stupid he is,* I think.

I have not moved yet but I am ready to try now. I wiggle my toes and fingers. The sun creeps over the cliff edge as the day is born. Sand must be removed from my nose and throat before I can answer him. Varno reads my mind and gingerly reaches his pinky into each nostril, the fingernail scraping away rough sand.

"Better now?"

His fingers reach into my mouth and pull out sand and shell fragments, pushing the smaller particles between my teeth.

"Please. Stop."

"Who pushed you over?" he says in a shaky voice.

I am too weak to tell him again to stop, so I close my eyes and shut everything out.

We lay together in the red foam while the sun creeps over the cliff and casts healing light on my arms and legs. Blood drips into the corner of my mouth and I put out my tongue for a taste.

I move my tongue around in my mouth, collecting and spitting out a coarse wad of sand. "Nobody. Pushed me. Do not be. Angry."

I hear him replaying my voice in his head. The blank face changes and tears form in the corners of his dark eyes.

I take deep breaths between my words. "I wanted. To. Die. But. I Could Not. Do it. Cannot do. Anything. Right."

I am done talking.

❧❧

All I want is to lie undisturbed on the crescent beach until I am bloodless and bone white, but my free will is lost to the caring of my tribe for their Three Face. I leapt into the water naked, but my honey-colored robe with the detailed beadwork is restored to me and my gashes are carefully cleaned. The acolytes wash all the sand from my hair as tears stream down their young faces. They are not much younger than I am but I feel worn down and used up in comparison.

I remember Mother telling me about her Spring Dreaming Ritual so long ago, and it made sense to me that she was overcome by the strength of the potion mixed by her tribe's Holy One. She did not know what was going to happen. Her young life had not prepared her for any of what came next.

But I should have been prepared for what can happen at a Spring Rite. As a Three Face, I mix the potions for the rites. I should know their strength. If I thought there was a possibility that my senses could be overcome at one of my own rites, I would have been drinking wild rue tea every day. I never worried. I do not understand how it happened.

I remember my surprise at realizing I was with child. Up until then I think I truly believed I was not a woman! I truly believed all my visions. What a rude awakening. What a deep embarrassment. What a fool!

Overwhelmed with the unworthiness of my condition, I took refuge in my cave with its soft sleeping furs and personal altar made from a large cluster of amethyst crystals, surrounded by smaller obsidian chunks and clear quartz points.

I refused to receive anyone and busied myself for days watching seabirds argue over dead fish and bits of crab. When I was tired I lay sleepless on my sleeping pallet, studying the ceremonial paintings on the ceiling and walls of my cave, recalling each rite and vision quest. I remember thinking, *I am supposed to be a Three Face. Not male, not female, not animal, yet all three, a Spirit talker. My magic will be broken now. No one will follow me.*

And I remember every day my acolytes brought savory broth and strips of dried meat to nourish me and my promise of life. Then, as the season warmed and the baby grew within me, they came with dandelion tea, sweet brown figs, and freshly grilled fish smelling delicious from the fire.

"You must eat! You are nurturing a child!" they laughed, shoving plates of food at me. They were enthusiastic and took turns spoiling me. With all my teaching and learning and visions, they were the ones who understood everything clearly.

As the weeks passed I must admit I became happy, even excited. Would it be a boy or a girl? I still believed in the importance of my vision quests and connection with animals, but the first time I felt the baby move I understood my true purpose. The women of the tribe celebrated by painting my latest vision on my growing belly: a baby, curled on its side, thumb in mouth, all ochre and blue.

I remember realizing I am not a Three Face. Realizing *there is no* Three Face. I fell in love with myself as a woman, ready to bring a new life to the Great Cliff tribe. I fell in love with my child before it was born.

As my time grew near I dreamt of an infant girl with wisps of yellow hair. I named her Shanara.

I went into labor before dawn. At first things progressed normally but as the hours passed it was clear the baby was in trouble. The women had seen this before; the cord was looped around the baby's neck. Each time I pushed to bring her forth, the cord pulled her back. If only they could get fingers around her head, they might slip the cord over or stretch it away. But I could not push hard enough. If I am a Three Face why did my visions not show me this? Why could the Spirits not guide my baby to daylight?

The labor went on through the day and night. A fire was lit so the women could see and water could be boiled. The elder women were brought up to my cave to assist the acolytes. There was more blood than I have ever seen as her slippery blue body was finally pulled out by Sora, the eldest and most skilled of the women. By then I was nearly comatose with exhaustion but I knew the baby had come. I was revived and ready to finally take my daughter into my arms!

My Shanara!

She looked so alone, curled on her side, lying on a golden hide in a sticky pool of my blood.

"A girl," said Sora, too quietly. She cut the cord away and immediately sucked the mucus from the baby's nose and mouth. Holding the slick newborn in her lap, she massaged the blue skin with sure strokes. Shanara's smoky eyes opened, she turned her face toward me, and emitted a weak cry.

Sora lifted her and I reached out eagerly, folding her to my heart. Kissing her everywhere. Cupping her in the palm of my hand. Supporting her head and neck with my fingers as she arched backward like a fish out of water.

"She cannot breathe," said Sora, with teeth clenched so tightly her lips barely moved.

I did not understand. The cord was cut and tied. The labor was over.

Sora was looking anywhere but at my face, as if she had something to tell me that she did not want to say. She bent down again, sucked hard at the baby's nose, and spat.

Shanara was warm against me and I wrapped my hands around her to keep in that warmth, feeling the delicate newness of her skin in wonderment, marveling at her mouth that was like the petals of a flower.

Delight in my daughter's utter perfection was shattered as her eyes squeezed shut and her body tensed in an effort to release another broken cry, fists flailing in frustration at what she was losing.

I began shaking uncontrollably. A queasy reality was trying to take me and I fought it. "Sora, what is happening?" I asked, trying to keep my voice even. "Why does she struggle?"

"Three Face, I do not know," she answered, almost mumbling. She slid her fingers tentatively around Shanara's little head and guided her tiny face toward my breast. "Perhaps she needs to suckle?" with doubt in her voice.

"How can she suckle when she cannot breathe!" My voice rose from my throat and I resisted the urge to tear at Sora like a wild animal. The elder woman could not look me in the eyes.

Cradling Shanara against my chest with one arm I pushed up into a sitting position. I held her face near mine and placed my lips tenderly over her nose and mouth so I could breathe in and out for her, not knowing if I did it right, trying to match her own breathing rhythm, realizing there was none.

"Beautiful girl." A whisper caught in my throat.

I remember when Varno pushed his way into the cave, panting hard. "What is happening?" his voice quivering and urgent.

"Shhh," said Sora. "This baby wants to sleep now."

I looked up at the old woman and was amazed to hear my voice issue from my throat like a roar. "What do you mean, sleep? She just got here!"

"Three Face, this baby is not ready to be born." This time Sora looked directly into my eyes when she spoke, hiding nothing.

I looked down to see Shanara gazing up at me as if in concentration. Her mouth pursed and her frail chest rose as she sucked in a ragged breath. Quickly I looked to Sora's blank face for reassurance, then put my attention back on the baby. "Yes, Shanara! Try!"

Still looking up at me with fists waving and tiny knees flexed, she managed another feeble cry. "Please," I whimpered, gently kissing her exquisite cheek, helplessly comforting her as she fought for air, terrified to feel her heart flutter like a broken wing.

Shanara's perfect fingers grabbed my forefinger and our eyes locked. Time stood still. I could not help but smile, and murmured, "Hello, sweet one."

A suggestion of a smile played across her mouth and her eyes closed. All her movements stopped though she still held my finger in her hand.

I looked frantically around the cave, searching to find someone who could help us. All the faces were wet with tears, all turning away, some sobbing loudly. Faces without bodies. Varno's face twisting as his mouth opened to cry out. And down to Shanara's face, tinged with blue, her hair contrasting with the skin like a circle of sunlight.

She was gone. She was dead.

Why should I be alive?

I sat sheltering her limp body against me, but Shanara grew cold. I rocked back and forth for hours while tears poured down my face and soaked into the front of my beaded honey-colored chamois robe.

People of the tribe moved in and out of my cave all day and into the night. Rows of crystal points encircled my fire, amplifying the flickering light with their purple or transparent facets. Many spoke in muted tones to me, bowing and turning away so they did not have to see their Three Face holding a dead baby in her arms.

They were like shadows to me.

Many hours later Sora came into the cave. I was dozing where I sat and woke with a start, trying to look as if I was awake all along.

"Three Face, I must take her now." The old hands reached down and carefully loosened Shanara's fragile body from my grasp. Sora and my acolytes silently left the cave, taking Shanara with them.

I was finally alone. The cave was serene with only the sounds of early evening to be heard. A falling leaf hitting the ground. Distant surf, and the dim tinkle of shells and pebbles turning and pulling with the tide. The weak pop of a coal dying on the fire.

Several cups of cold tea sat beside my sleeping pallet. The fire burned down to embers. The crystal points went dark. The paintings on the ceiling became indistinct. Through the mouth of the cave I saw the last of a setting sun.

And in that moment of peace I understood there was no reason for me to live another day.

I sob and cry out loud while I lie alone on the ground in a cool forest of trees with beautiful sienna bark and deep green leaves. I can hardly see anymore because my eyes are so swollen, but when

I glance down at my hands the skin is dry and the blue veins stand out under pale skin.

There is no sign of Shanara and I am no longer Astara. The rest of that life is behind me. I know I'm Evie again and I will never regain anything I've lost.

The bottomless sadness, frustration and emptiness is familiar to me but I'm not sure why. Astara's life was filled with the challenge of staying alive and her path was often lonely and separate from those she loved, but she was a person of action. Frustration was never a big part of her life.

I return to my mind and start searching for an answer.

Crying to the point of exhaustion is familiar to me, but why? My clinical thought process is instantly infuriating. Is this who Evie is? A person who cries from the depth of her soul one minute and the next minute begins to analyze her actions like an automaton?

I was never this robotic, was I? My heart and soul are hurting. During my life as Evie I never knew why I hurt so much. I chalked my pain up to things my parents said and did, things I was prevented from doing, friends I never had or couldn't keep, love I never found and then lost.

My time as Astara was an incredible gift! I realize I am first and foremost a *soul* who has been graced with time on Earth, living the human drama as best as I can. Astara was my first time at the exercise of life, and what a woman she was! Without framework, without knowledge or support, Astara carved her way with her own teeth and nails into a human sculpture, climbing her life like it was the killing cliff face where she tried to make an end to the pain of losing a child. Love for her lost child devastated her heart and she believed she could not go on living as a human who would always be in pain.

This seems to be the human legacy – trying to find love, finding it or not, losing it, and living in pain.

I'm ashamed to say my life as Evie doesn't seem to have progressed my soul much further along than Astara's life did. Eons later, with all the advances humanity has made, I came into the world without direction, made my way ineptly and without wisdom, looking for what – Love? Can I say that now, lying in the forest, looking through swollen eyes to find the sky?

Yes, I *do* say it! My soul was created knowing about the secrets of the heart, about loving others, about loving myself. Only in living did I forget how to love.

But it's all right. There is no one to please here. The trees are not standing in judgment of me. They don't even know I'm here. I am inconsequential. There is no one to disappoint. I can be myself. Honesty is not a liability here.

Whose voice am I hearing? I remember it, one of a young woman. Is it something I heard when I sat so many times in my cave cross-legged with eyes closed, hearing only the sounds of the sea crashing endlessly in the dark?

I have been sitting in the dark for a long time. My mind at this moment is the kind of blank I tried to reach during my time as a Three Face. Perhaps I have reached the place I was meant to go after all, to a future place where I tried to lead my tribe.

What will happen when I lay out my life before myself? Which life am I talking about? I remember a fulfilled and complete life by the sea, until Shanara.

Think! Feel! You are a Three Face. You can understand anything shown to you.

And then I remember. There is no such thing as a Three Face. There is only a small, insignificant human, making her naked way through life, chasing visions of who she thinks she is, and devastated by the death of her newborn child. Astara fought to be a Three Face, and then came to the conclusion her mind had made it all up. But at least she believed in something for a while.

I lie quietly where I fell among familiar scents of the forest, and something comes to me that I have seen before. A woman's life in a place with loud noises and tall structures, surrounded by countless people and constant movement.

I dreamed that life the night before I left the Golden Fish tribe and sometimes glimpsed it on vision quests as a Three Face. It was not imagined, it was my real life in another place and time.

It was a vision of my life as Evelyn, a woman of the future.

CHAPTER ELEVEN

I'm starting to think I will never move of my own accord again. I fall into a reverie, reviewing images flashing before my eyes, faster, faster, now blurring into a golden hard seed like a single kernel of corn or a bud of wheat. A streamlined capsule of promise containing an entire life, needing the right conditions to unfurl and grow! That's it in a nutshell! A golden seed. A life.

My life as Evelyn – the 21st Century life I left behind – why even bother to remember it? It is already lived and over. There's nothing to unfurl, no promise.

My life. Graceless. Confused. A story of an ordinary girl. I was a helpless baby once, a child born to adoring parents who wanted to give me everything good. Good food. Good place to live. Good family.

It's not a new story. A small baby begins walking and reaching. She wants to know what everything is, how it works, how it fits into the world of herself, Mommy and Daddy, living in the suburbs of New York City in the 1950s. The baby starts to speak, everyone is dying for her to say Mama and Dada, and it's cute at first.

Then come my many questions. I remember the answers, ask more questions, and my mind builds a beautiful world. I am happy, learning about everything with excitement and a feeling of accomplishment as things begin to make more sense every day. I wake up with music taking form inside and release it with maximum joy each morning, sending it out from my soul to my parents, my dreams, and my books and toys. I make up songs for everything in my home. Singing connects me to all of life so I am not alone. I am very noisy and busy making songs for the Universe I see all around me.

But sources of non-joy lie like traps everywhere. I want to share my special joy with my parents, but they seem to have lost their connection. Mommy never stops cooking, cleaning and making sure she is dressed every day like we're going out somewhere. She's so beautiful! Daddy does things every day that make him frown or fall asleep on the couch at night. On the weekends when he is home my parents like to sleep very late. Sleep is a treat for them. I don't understand why they are so tired.

I stand in the doorway of their bedroom and call to them tentatively, toys in hand, ready to play a game. "Mommy? Daddy? I want to show you something, okay?"

All they can say is, "Hush now, Evelyn We're still sleeping. Let Mommy and Daddy rest now. Go play quietly in your room."

They don't even move when they talk to me. Are they talking to someone who lives in their pillows? I move to their bed to see better, but they roll over onto their sides, facing away. I remember from one of my books or something someone said: Children should be seen and not heard.

Is that true? With a shock, I realize nobody wants to hear me.

My parents don't want me to come into their room to show them how my toys play together, and the songs we sing. They've told me what they want: be quiet until they wake up, hours away! Everything I think is wonderful turns out to be bad, when all I want is to be good. It takes some time but after being scolded or ignored morning after morning, I stop myself from singing. I still sing of course, but very softly. I don't visit Mommy and Daddy in their bedroom anymore because they are not happy to see me and they don't like the games I invent. I'm told girls don't invent games. Good Girls play with miniature kitchens and tea sets and are quiet until someone speaks to them.

I learn to move on quiet toes in the mornings. I whisper my songs so I can barely hear them myself. I wait to go to the bathroom so I will not make noise. I am good, not only in the morning, but all day. I know how to play with my toys quietly in my room while Mommy takes a nap. Why does she sleep so much anyway? There is much I don't understand but I desperately need approval from the people I love.

Love means me being quiet and doing nothing. It means being out of the way. It's all I want. I will do anything to have it.

Finally! I am good and quiet. They wake up, stumbling to put on their clothes. Will they play with me now? No, Daddy wants to make the special breakfast only he can make on Saturday and Sunday. He's the creative one, the artist in the family, and art and perfection extend to breakfast in our home. Bacon, round pancakes, eggs with the yellow mound jiggling exactly in the middle, all perfect. Breakfast doesn't interest me but I attempt to sit quietly at the table. When will breakfast be over so I can go outside? I'll see if anyone next door wants to play a game. Anything but breakfast. But instead I'm stuck at the table doing Saturday and Sunday things.

The egg smells horrible, the bacon is crunchy and salty enough to pucker my cheeks, and I pull apart the thick brown pancakes so I can see the bubbles inside. I'm not hungry and ask Daddy where the pancake bubbles come from, but he is not interested in answering questions. He wants me to eat the pancakes. I try to tell Daddy I will eat them if I can melt butter over the bubbles while they're still hot, but nobody is listening.

"May I please have some butter?" I ask in the polite way I've been taught. This receives no answer although Daddy glares at me for a full two seconds.

Maybe they didn't hear or understand me; I'm only four years old and my words may not be coming out right.

"May I have some butter? Please?" I try to look cute, sliding my eyes from Mommy to Daddy and smiling while I kick my feet back and forth against the chair to make it jump. I keep hearing I have 'big hazel eyes', whatever they are, and my looks get a lot of attention from my aunts, who stroke my hair and talk about my 'coloring'.

Mommy and Daddy are eating now, pushing at the disgusting yellow egg with buttered toast. It's not fair. They get butter and I don't.

"Don't use it all up! I need butter!"

"Josie, what is she saying? Make her sit still, will you?" Daddy's handsome mouth changes to a line that turns down at both ends, stiff and tired.

It is only morning with eggs and pancakes but Daddy's thick black hair is perfectly combed and smoothed down with a gel that smalls nice. He's already shaved and he even put out his cigarette so he can sit at the table properly. Daddy wants me sitting on the chair eating quietly as if I were part of a painting of breakfast.

"Frank, the child may not like eggs and pancakes. Let me make her some cereal."

Mommy turns to me with a voice almost like singing. "How about some nice Cream of Wheat?"

She gets up from her chair, walks two steps to the cupboard with a hard clap clap of her high heeled shoes, and pokes toward the yellow box on the shelf with long red nails. Somehow between waking up late and fumbling with clothes, she has put on a dress for breakfast along with pretty shoes and those see-through socks called stockings. I am very sure I will never wear those. They don't look comfortable. I've seen how Mommy twists and pulls to get them on while she's getting dressed. And those white plastic round things with metal on the back side to hold everything up leave red marks on her legs. If that's growing up, I don't want any part of it.

Mommy is already at the stove with the yellow box and water in a pot. "No Mommy, I don't want Cream of Wheat!" I whine, throw my head back, roll my eyes, and jangle my legs harder against the chair.

I'm getting taller now; they say I'm tall for four years old, going through another 'growth spurt'. My long brown hair is pulled back into a ponytail that is badly tangled because I run away when I know Mommy is going to work on the knots. It hurts when she digs her nails into my scalp trying to hold me still while she tugs at my hair!

"The child needs a haircut, Josie. She looks like a gypsy," Daddy says.

"We can do that later," she answers, and to me, "Eat your food, Evelyn. You need your nourishment," as if I am starving, and as if I haven't been ready to eat my pancakes if only someone would pass the butter.

I sense it will not go well if I don't eat something. I pick at the dry, pulled-apart piece of pancake, fold it around a broken chunk of bacon and stick it in my mouth. I chew noisily thinking, *this is pretty good.* I will eat anything rather than a solidified bowl of white Cream of Wheat that looks like plastic, sprinkled with some of that brown stuff from a jar called cinnamon. It's dusty and makes me sneeze. Once Cream of Wheat gets cold it turns into a plastic drum that you have to cut with a knife.

Nice house, doting parents, my own room, toys, lots of clothes, cousins to play with, neighbor kids from other houses on the block to be friends with.

But I am so lonely. I want a real friend, someone *important* in my life. Why can't there be two of us? I sit outside on the huge bolder next to the garden and look into the other yards, singing out loud to fill empty space with another voice besides the one in my head.

"Hello," says my song, "are you the other one?" My supple voice rises high and pure. The dogs in the neighborhood are attracted to me and visit every afternoon. Looking back, my voice was probably a special call that only they could hear! I love their wet noses and velvet ears, and the way they lie in the grass breathing in the beautiful blue and silver air of summer, panting and smiling as they rest their sides against me.

The kids who come by are another story. Tommy is my next-door neighbor and best friend whom I love dearly. But I am afraid of most of the other kids on the block because the bigger boys have invented a horrible game and everyone follows the big boys. They chase after cats, trying to grab their tails so they can whirl them around fast and then let them go, screaming and clawing through the air. Those boys don't like me because I won't play their game, and tell them what they are doing is wrong. They laugh at me and say, "What's wrong with it? They're just cats!" And they imitate me when I sing, like I'm strange.

The dogs, the cats, the kids. None of these is the other one I'm looking for.

And then there is a whisper: Mommy is going to have a baby! I think back to the dreamlike time of my childhood and I don't recall my mother ever being pregnant. Does she try to hide it? That sounds like my parents. Anything regarding the body is dirty and embarrassing. But no matter how she feels about it, the pregnancy progresses month by month until one day Mommy leaves for the hospital and a day later she comes home again as if nothing happened. But something *must* have happened.

The questions spill out of me. "Where's the baby? Is it a boy or a girl?" I'm excited, expectant, so ready to no longer be the lonely girl. I plead so they will tell me where the baby is. I whine, I whisper, "When can I see it? Is it okay?"

Low voices and furtive looks from my parents give me no answers. There is still no baby. But I'm told there will be, soon. If I'm good. If I'm quiet.

And then Yes, there is a baby! It's a girl! My new sister is named after Daddy's grandma, a woman he loved and respected more than anyone else in his life. The baby's name is Liliana.

Daddy's grandma died a long time before I was born so I never met her, but I know what she looked like from a charcoal portrait Daddy made that hangs on our living room wall. In the portrait she's old and taut as a spring, the tendons of her neck standing out and her gray-white hair pulled back with a dark kerchief to showcase a careworn but proud expression. Sharp Roman eyes are like black birds flying out at your face.

She outlived all her husbands and all her children during the Great Depression in a New York City tenement that froze in winter and steamed in summer. Grandma Liliana raised three grandsons with no money except whatever pennies she made scrubbing down the building where they lived on Eldridge Street. Daddy talks about going to 6 a.m. Mass with her every morning, then picking up rags and broken pieces of wood on their way home so they could have a fire to keep warm and cook their food. There was no help from Daddy's alcoholic father after Daddy's mother – Grandma Liliana's daughter – was found dead in the street at age thirty-eight.

Grandma's picture is scary like the times she lived through. Daddy tells the story about how she used a broom and potent Italian curses to chase away the men from the Foundling Home when they came to take away her young grandsons. That was after Daddy's mother died and there was only Grandma and the boys' father, drunk and abusive. Grandma cursed Daddy's father – my grandpa – after her daughter died, telling him he would "blow up like a blowfish". And he did! My grandpa was terrified of Grandma Liliana and her curses long after she was dead. He told us he would wake up in the middle of the night to see her ghost standing at the foot of his bed, cursing him from her grave.

I hope it was true. It sounds like he deserved it. I wish I had known her. Even at a young age I couldn't take my eyes off her portrait. Her eyes seemed to follow me no matter where I was in the room.

My attention returns to the present. My parents are explaining my sister Liliana has been born but is staying in the hospital because she is pree-mah-choor and weak. She's living in some kind of box, an in-kew-bay-tor.

"What's pree-mah-choor?" I ask as though I can gather power over this new word.

Mommy gives information with clear enunciation. "Say the word correctly dear. Pre-ma-*ture*. It means she is still very small. She'll stay in the incubator until she gets a little bigger."

She's finished giving information and reaches to the ashtray for her ever-lit cigarette, which she sucks on deeply before blowing out again, receding behind the comfort of smoke.

"What's Liliana's nickname?" I ask. "Mine's Evie; what's hers?" I feel better asking about this than about the box Liliana is living in.

"We'll call her Lilly." Like a flower.

Is Lilly sick? Why is she living in a box? Why are my parents always whispering? Why aren't they more excited about the new baby? The questions whirl around in my head and there are no answers. All I can say to myself is *Lilly, come home! Get stronger. I'll take care of you!*

Lilly spends a long time in an incubator. As I recall it was probably several weeks, or a month, or even longer. Because nobody speaks about what is going on I understand this is serious. Lilly only weighs around four pounds. I have not seen my sister yet, but I know she is kept in a plastic box so she can stay alive, and there are tubes, and nobody can touch her, and she is being kept very warm. My parents do not give me much information but I hear Mommy talking to Aunt Letty every day and I hear all the scary new words. My parents are like sleep walking zombies who float in and out of our house, coming and going with no explanation. My Aunt Gracie lives closer than Aunt Letty and comes to stay with me in the afternoons.

"Are Mommy and Daddy at the hospital with Liliana?"

"I don't know Evelyn. They don't tell me." Aunt Gracie makes dinner for us and smiles a lot but doesn't say much. When I start to ask questions, she tells me to "Ask your Mommy and Daddy when they come home." There are no answers, but I am not afraid. I have not experienced anything bad in my life yet, so I cannot imagine they will allow anything bad to happen to Lilly.

And then Lilly comes home and I am no longer a lonely, skinny kid looking for something. I find my sister at last!

Judging from each day of my life since the day she came home I know it is one of the best days in my life. I must have been ecstatic! But I don't remember it.

What kind of person doesn't remember the best day of their life?

What I *do* remember is that once my sister comes home I am totally in love.

I am still down here with the sweet rotten things, making a comfortable dent in the soft loam. I am able to completely review each moment in my recalled life and there is so much good. A huge and defining love covers and breathes into me.

My life wasn't lonely after all, it was a life filled with love. That's what I remember as I recline here among pinecones. Sure, my parents weren't the most interested in my creative pursuits. It was the time I grew up in I guess – the vast cultural and intellectual wasteland of the 1950s – and it was the character of my family. Girls weren't expected to do much more than smile all the time and be attractive, become women, get married to a successful guy, and have two or three perfect children.

All a women's activities revolved around doing things for the family. An acceptable career for a woman was teaching, so she could have a job to go back to once her children got older, or being a receptionist in a doctor's office so she could make some 'pin money' on the side. The man's work was the important thing. The woman's real career was to marry a man with a good job in a corporation, or a man with skills who belonged to a good union.

A girl's important skills didn't come from reading or doing well in school. They were honed from birth to enable her to find a successful man and get married. Her very serious career was to look good, smile and be happy, and keep herself pure for the man who would create her life for her.

Her skill sets were 'feminine wiles' in which she always complimented any man, and told every man that he was smart and strong and handsome. She must develop skills as a homemaker so she could cook nourishing and delicious meals for her family even on the strictest budget. She had to know how to buy the best food at the lowest prices, keep the house spotless, and make her husband proud of how she looked when they went out somewhere.

That's the good life my parents want for me and Mommy works hard to teach me how to fit into this pre-programmed role. She explains it's no different than young girls being groomed for their role in life anyplace else, like Pakistan or Africa or even Old World Italy, except that of course being in America is much better than being anyplace else. We are free here in America. All the immigrants trying desperately to Anglicize themselves come from backward places without running water like Italy, Greece, Spain, and Portugal. Then you have the Stone Age places like Iran, Arabia, Egypt, Turkey, and all those countries where women are covered head to toe, paint designs on their hands, wear nose rings with chains attached from nostril to ear, and get married when they are still children. Or I could have ended up in Africa where there is nothing except bushes with thorns, wild animals, and people wearing no clothes.

Growing up as a small child in America in the 1950s is like being in a dream where everyone is always smiling and mothers wear aprons while holding a wooden spoon. Get up, go to school, come home, do homework, eat dinner, watch shows on that newest thing – the TV – play with friends, go on vacation, get older each year and repeat the cycle with newer, more grown-up clothes.

As if I'm struck with an electric shock I start jerking around right here where I lie. I remember the 1950s now, and not fondly! It's a time when everything in my life is monitored. I am a young half-Italian, half-Greek girl who is under surveillance by the family, being groomed for my future life as a woman. I am an outdoor-loving child being dragged along kicking and screaming toward an inevitable future of acceptable behavior and emotions.

But I am not domesticated. At ages six through ten I am in my glory playing with my friends, who are all boys. They are easy to talk to and more fun than the girls. The boys don't compare their clothes and toys to mine. They don't ask a lot of questions and they don't laugh at me when I give the wrong answer about clothes or dolls. They don't even talk about those things. Boys explore the neighborhood and wander in the woods. Together we climb and crawl and play Cowboys and Indians.

I remember my Roy Rogers jacket made of soft tan suede, with long suede tassels hanging from wrists to arm pits. I run my hand over that suede a million times – dark, light, dark, light, and soft, soft, soft! I love that jacket. The pockets are deep and lined in more suede, perfect for collecting special acorns or for cradling small orange salamanders I sometimes find in muddy lots where new houses are starting to be built.

In the warm weather everyone's Dad puts up a plastic above-ground pool in the back yard where we kids play and keep cool. I hate wearing a lot of clothes when the summer gets hot and humid. Long before Lilly comes, when I am very young, we run though lawn sprinklers. When we get bigger we're ready for the pool. I hate school and love every long bright day of summer. I love the sweat and the heat and how my skin tingles in the sunshine. I pedal my blue Schwinn bike as fast as I can down our hill, and in August when it's really hot we wear practically nothing to play outside. Nobody is worried about their outfit. I'm tan all over, taller than most of the other kids on the block, all legs and arms right up until I'm twelve years old.

Then I stop growing and start turning into a woman, and suddenly I have to wear a lot of clothes. But that's all in the future. Now I'm the leader on the block, the strongest at arm wrestling, the best at scatter dodge ball, the fastest runner. No one can jump as high as me. Being a kid is made for me.

Unfortunately, these are not skills that will take me into womanhood. No matter what Mom says I can't seem to learn how to sit in one place, keep my clothes clean, and tell boys they are smart and strong.

"Why can't you *sit* in a chair?" Mom frowns at my scrawny legs bent in opposite directions, strewn over the arm and cushion of her dark green velvet couch with the yellow piping. "Sit like a lady. Here, let me show you."

She places her lips into a pout shape at the same time that she lines up her backside with the couch cushion and lowers herself slowly downward, bending at the knees while her arms are out at her sides kind of waving like she's doing a ballet dance. I wonder what a pout face has to do with sitting down more like a lady, but I don't ask.

"Now you try it," her voice filled with hope that her awkward child can improve.

I don't know how to pout and lower myself slowly. I line my backside up with the cushion and fling myself backward with a big sigh and swinging arms.

"What did I show you Evelyn? When are you ever going to learn? When you get older the boys won't like you."

No amount of coaching gets me to stop flopping onto the couch. I don't feel right doing it her way. I feel like I'm going crazy.

Mom puts a lot of restrictions on the things I can do. Now I understand she is afraid some harm will come to me so it would be best if I didn't do anything. She is constantly sticking phrases like *you musn't* and *you can't* and *Good Girls don't* in front of everything I want to do.

"Mom, the ice cream man's here! Can I have orange ices? Or a Creamsicle?"

"No dear, you mustn't. You'll get a sore throat."

No matter that it's 102 degrees and the middle of August.

"Mom, I want a horse! Can we get one? We have a lawn so it will have plenty of room there. It can live in my room. You always say my room looks like a stable. I want to learn to ride like Dale Evans on Buttermilk and Roy Rogers on Trigger. Mom, *please?*"

"We've talked about this over and over. You know you *mustn't* ride, it's a very dangerous sport. If you fall the horse will trample you and you will be paralyzed for life! You'll break your neck! Please don't do this to me!"

"Mom, can I take singing lessons this year instead of piano? Please? You know how I always want to sing."

"Your father and I have told you many times Evelyn, *Good Girls don't* become singers! Singers are drug addicts and loose women! They are low-class people and they die young. It's not for you dear! They're not our kind of people. I'm sorry, but you'll end up addicted to drugs. You don't want to be found dead in the streets, do you? You'll thank me some day."

How did I buy into all these restrictions? I suppose it happens to everyone. We all want to fit in and please our parents, teachers, friends. After hearing over and over again about how everything I want to do is dangerous and how only bad people do the things I want to do, I start believing it. Why would my parents lie to me? I am being ungrateful as usual. They are protecting me. They love me. Everyone says so. There must be something wrong with me for wanting to do all those crazy, dangerous things.

I know they love me. But it feels like they're forcing me into a mold that doesn't fit.

And then a bright spot opens up when Liliana comes home. I'm nine going on ten that year. There are many ways for me to love my sister, to see her lovely skin so translucent and alive, to play games with her and make her laugh. She does anything with me. I think she idolizes me because I'm her big sister.

My joy at having this small perfect being in my life is unimaginable and endless. I am constantly hovering around my mother, wanting to hold the baby, wanting to help take care of her, smell her, touch her.

I am not allowed to take care of her at all. Mom is like a large buffeting cloud, carefully ensconcing the tiny waving hands with the strong curve of her shoulder and arm, brushing Lilly's dark hair upward into a kewpie doll point using the world's softest brush with bristles like fairy strands, stoically rinsing cloth diapers, and rocking my baby sister to sleep. Lilly seems to love when Mom sings to her. I always hated it; something about the theatrical way she moves her face, as if everyone is watching, as if she is somebody else.

"You can hold her later, when she's stronger."

"When will she be stronger?"

"Soon dear." Mommy speaks quietly as though this life is not real, as if she is in a dream. She reaches for another cigarette as soon as Liliana is asleep in her crib. I can feel her vibrate and sigh with release as she inhales deeply and blows out a huge stale cloud.

As life with Lilly progresses I am happy and involved although I'm not allowed to handle her very much, and at the same time I know something is not right. I know because my mother knows. Although it has been nearly nine years between babies, she remembers. At three months they try to turn over. At four months they turn onto their tummies. Their heads and necks become strong. Their grasp is sure and curious. At six months their eyes lock onto whatever is around them and they want to put it in their mouth. They start getting white buds of teeth pushing up through their pink gums. They smile directly at you and their movements are more and more controlled. They reach out their hands with purpose and they don't let go. You can see them memorizing everything.

Lilly is slow to turn, and her movements are slightly spastic as if she doesn't have full command of her muscles. She smiles a lot, but we aren't always sure she is smiling at us. I am not bothered by these details. I am so happy I am no longer alone. I know she is smiling at me. I can feel her like a little dart pointing at me, following me, exploring and knowing my face, my eyes, delighting in this bigger person who is outside of herself but with her always. Loving me.

I hear Mommy and Daddy talking at night with low voices. I stop breathing and let the whispers lie heavy on my ears.

"Frank."

"Yes, Josie."

"I don't know, there's something about the baby."

"No Josie. It's fine. They would have said. Go to sleep."

"They don't know Frank. I know. She should have been crawling by now."

"There's nothing to worry about, Jo. Go back to sleep."

My parents become quiet, but their voices repeat in my mind. And I know Mommy is right. Something is wrong with Lilly.

The winter wears on. It's been cold and Liliana is not always well. Whispers and quick movement in the hallway awaken me some nights. I get out of bed quietly and lean into Lilly's room; nobody notices me. My mother has Lilly in her lap, she is bent over intently, holding the baby in her two hands under the lamp light. Liliana wheezes pathetically, rhythmically. The pink fists wave but she can't even cry.

I slide into the room, ready to help. We don't know what's wrong and why she is so sick, but we fight to help her breathe. I hold her face steady near the humidifier. Mommy bends over Liliana with something she calls an "atomizer" to suck the congestion out of the baby's head and clear her enough to take a breath. One squeeze of the atomizer. One gasp of breath. This baby may be weak, but she's a fighter. We fight too, to keep her alive.

Mommy takes such good care of Liliana. On the nights when the baby gets all stuffed up and needs help breathing she's always there, steady and calm, determined to help her child. As Lilly gets older and more mischievous she is always so patient, and never loses her temper with Lilly no matter what mess she makes or what she does wrong. Mommy does everything to keep Lilly safe, healthy and happy. I will always love that about her. Even if she didn't do any of those things for me.

Or she did, and I just don't remember.

Months pass, warmer weather comes, Lilly continues smiling but progress in other areas is slow. When she reaches nine months old Lilly can finally turn over on her own, some of the time. Other times I'm there to help her turn over. My mother says nothing about her worries. The rest of the family is encouraging and dotes on the gorgeous child with the translucent skin, dark eyes and walnut brown hair.

But there is a stiffness to Mommy's jaw now. She sucks in one cigarette after another and a constant black coffee sits like a cup of tar on the kitchen table while the pot perks, a portable volcano on the stove. All her concentration is on my sister, keeping my sister alive.

I am completely happy to wheel Lilly around in her carriage with me whenever I am allowed. All my friends love her because she is so small and beautiful like a china doll come to life, and she is always laughing. I hold her hands as she tries to stand on her feet and walk. Always her direct brown eyes look deep into mine, no blinking or looking away. She is a bold child, unaware that she is weak and small. We are connected. She seems to love everyone and everything.

And the summer turns to autumn, the leaves turn colors, it gets colder, the leaves fall down dead. My favorite holidays come and go and I don't notice. Have Daddy and Mommy stopped speaking except to say the necessary things?

Mommy is animated when other people are around, accenting her speech with the elegance of red fingernails while a lit cigarette held between her lips flaps up and down with each word. She's a mixed media of grace and coarseness that attracts and repels me at the same time. She is always beautifully dressed, and her red hair and polished fingernails along with her open personality make her stand out. The holidays bring music and company to our home. Mommy makes a huge prime rib roast and lasagna. We visit my aunts on the Lower East Side in the city.

Every time we go into Chinatown for dinner the people stare at us, a wagon train of loud Mediterranean people with three children trailing behind. There's my cousin Fred, dark and flaccid. Me skinny, sullen and tanned with big hazel eyes and my honey brown hair chopped off now in an embarrassing style my father approvingly calls the Italian Boy, and my friends call the Bald Eagle. Leave it to my parents to give me a boy's haircut. And then there's my sister Liliana in a stroller, looking like an expensive porcelain doll that moves. Shiny dark hair, pale delicate skin, turned-up nose, and slanted dark brown eyes. She looks like she was born in Chinatown. The people on the street stare in fascination at the beautiful child with the loud family.

It's January and Liliana is finally a year old. The respiratory issues seem to be improving and we go to the doctor for Lilly's one-year-old checkup. He greets my parents like old friends, and the family is ushered into the examination room. That is, all but me. The doctor leads me into an empty room in the complex, turns to me with a *you stay here young*

lady while I speak to your parents, and then he closes the door and locks it!

I'm left alone in an examination room. The lights are off but there is a window onto the street that allows light to enter. I don't want to sit on anything in case a hidden doctor might jump out and try to examine me or stick me with a needle. I stand in the center of the room, turning around slowly to see the table with stiff white paper over it, the sink with a soap dispenser and medical instruments in a container on the counter. The room smells of Mercurochrome with an undertone of cigar. One wall has an interior glass window with venetian blinds pulled down. I don't dare touch them to see where I am in relation to my parents and Liliana. There is a faint noise of typing coming from the receptionist area and no other noise.

I feel very hurt in this room. There is nothing a doctor can do to heal the hurt that comes from being put in this room. I hate the doctor for putting me here. Why did my parents allow him to take me away and place me alone, away from the family? They probably don't even know where I am now. A tight red burning starts in my belly. Am I getting sick from being locked in this room with medicine smells? The only thing that helps is walking around in circles.

A long while later the doctor comes back, opens the door, says nothing, and leads me back to my parents. They are in the main part of the office now, putting on coats and hats. The doctor visit is over. Nobody is speaking to me to see how I am and where I've been, and nobody is talking to each other. The doctor looks grave and shakes Daddy's hand, like they've made a deal.

Mommy is trying to dress Liliana in her pink hat and coat so we can leave the office while Lilly squirms and tries to reach out for me instead, but I am standing apart from everyone, struggling to get my arm into my coat.

I want to sob and cry but I hold my breath to keep it all in. I open my eyes wide to stop the tears from falling, and clench my teeth to stop my chin from trembling. My belly is tied into a red-hot knot, and all I want is to move now to get rid of the feeling, to run away and break something with a loud noise. But being a *Good Girl*, I have no such outlet. The doctor visit is over and life is about to go on.

Our family leaves the office with Mommy holding Lilly in her arms. I trail along, dragging my feet noisily on the sidewalk all the while shifting my shoulders inside my coat which I still haven't gotten on right. Being able to move now is helping with the burning in my belly, but my brain is still red with questions. Daddy takes big steps like he is in a rush to get away from something. Mommy, who is normally able to find something to talk about no matter what, says nothing.

The silence is killing me. "What's wrong with my sister?" I call to my parents as the question burns a hole in my brain. I'm afraid even to speak, as if saying the word *wrong* will make it true. I have been absolutely terrified since the doctor locked me in that room.

"What's wrong with my sister?"

Mommy always wears high-heeled shoes to make herself taller, and to go with her perfect outfits. Now her beautiful legs reach out and back, out and back, in crazy precision. The narrow heels strike sharply on the sidewalk one after the other and she bounces with each step. I catch a waft of her perfume – Stradivari by Prince Machabelli with the bottle that looks like a glass crown. I think she is probably having a fit because she can't smoke while she's holding Lilly.

Daddy looks like something bad has happened, but nobody will say what it is. Did I do something wrong? No, that can't be it, nobody's paying attention to me. Daddy looks gray and his face pulls into his neck, making him flat like a stone fort moving on legs, with eyes like black slits in a tower you can't reach, where arrows could come flying out at any moment and pierce into your heart.

What did that doctor do to my parents?

No one speaks. No one answers. They walk faster and I run to keep up, off balance on spindly legs and stiff patent-leather shoes as my parents move quickly along the sidewalk.

"What's wrong with my sister?"

I look from Mommy to Daddy, and then to Liliana who reaches happily toward me with her perfect hands. I'm starting to feel the hot belly again. Lilly looks fine to me. Mommy is still walking fast. Daddy says nothing. He looks like someone died.

"Okay! What's wrong with my sister?" I stop walking and yell, as loud as I dare, with a weak hope that my question will get through to people who are acting crazy and deaf. My voice has a new

tang to it that showed up on its own, like I have no control anymore over myself.

"It's nothing honey," Mommy sighs, square shoulders slumping under the tweed coat as if the bones have gone out of her. "It's just that she's not as smart as other babies. She's what they call Mentally Retarded."

I wait for more. I wait to hear something terrifying, something life-threatening, something that makes sense with how they are acting. But that's all there is.

Strike, strike, strike, the high heeled shoes punish the sidewalk and nobody says another word about it.

I explode with relief. *"Is that all?"* I shout. The burning subsides. I'm filled with a sudden joy. I forget about the doctor's office. I jump up and down like I'm on a pogo stick, filled with energy, pawing up at Lilly's hand. "I thought she was going to die!" I hold back tears that were ready to fall and are now unnecessary. Liliana starts to laugh at me. I must look funny with my skinny legs and short hair flapping up and down, pushing away a few stray tears.

My worst fears evaporate into the air. Lilly is not sick. She is not going to die. She's just retarded, whatever that is. Who cares if she's not as smart as other babies? She seems smart to me. She's okay! She's going to be okay!

I am drunk with joy and relief and the burning is gone and I don't care about mentally retarded anything. But I see that they care. My parents care. My father, especially, cares.

Years pass and love grows. Liliana and I have a special bond. Everyone comments on how close we are, on how 'good' I am with her, on how I understand her and help her negotiate her way through times when she is not well understood by others. So many pictures fly through my mind like impressions in the water, here for a moment and then rippling away.

Lilly lies in my lap with her face looking up. "Ahhhhh," she says, like a happy song. I take my hand and pat her mouth to create a doppler effect, and she says *ah* for as long as she can until we both dissolve into happy laughter. She always laughs from her heart. I can tell she has access to parts of herself we supposedly smarter people have lost. She always operates from the depths of her soul. Life is a simple joy to her.

Lilly runs haphazardly on the grass, spinning round and round with her head thrown back, tasting sunlight and making herself dizzy, tripping and laughing, always laughing.

Lilly rests her head on my lap in the evening, looks up at me as her eyes grow heavy, twirls her hair around her fingers, and then falls asleep with a light and even breath sucking on her two middle fingers.

She always laughs such a true and important laugh. Important for me, since I never seem to do anything right except with Lilly. As I get older it gets worse. Mom is always yelling at me, telling me not to do the things I want so desperately to do.

Everything is off limits and my activities are monitored. Dad is stern and defends every restriction, telling me to "Listen to your mother! She's very smart. She knows what she's talking about!"

But Liliana is a bright light. Her dark eyes lock with mine and she seems like the boldest, wisest person in the world. I have someone of my own to love. Finally. And it seems she loves me back.

She's older, she's walking and talking, at least her version of talking. As she struggles to form words and sentences to tell us what she is thinking and feeling, I am her faithful translator. I have a lot of patience. I can spend a long time repeating the sounds she makes as she uses gestures and cute expressions to illustrate what she is telling us. She often has something emphatic to say, and other times the mundane things of life take her a long time to get us to understand.

"Kwakee," says Lilly.

"Kwakee," I repeat back. "Is it a person?"

"No. Kwakee."

"Okay. I know. Kwakee. Show me what you mean. It is food?"

"Yeth."

"Is it breakfast?"

"No. Kwakee."

She points to the refrigerator freezer. "Kwakee!"

"Ice cream?" A good guess since it's her favorite food apart from bacon with mustard.

"Yeth. Kwakee!"

"Kwakee – chocolate! Of course!"

"Yeth! Kwakee!"

"Okay. I got it! You want chocolate ice cream." And she sits down expecting a big bowl of her favorite food. We are so relieved! Another difficult transaction successfully executed.

That's how things go for a few years, one small step at a time, life through life. Milestones, side by side, me holding her hand to let her know I will always be there.

Dad seems to get over his initial shock at finding out Lilly is mentally retarded. The more correct term is she was born with Down Syndrome. Nobody knows exactly why it happened. Maybe because Mom was 40 years old when she became pregnant, or maybe because of her heavy smoking – three packs a day – or maybe the luck of the draw. The medical profession is not very knowledgeable.

"Don't worry Frank, she won't live long," the doctor assured Dad.

The doctors don't understand Down people can live as long and do all the same things everyone else does, though they might need some help. Based on medical ignorance, the doctors counsel my parents to put Lilly away in a facility and forget about her.

"It's the best thing for everybody, Frank."

But that is not going to happen.

"What are you, *crazy*, Josephine? Nobody in *this* family is going to be *put away* in an *institution!*"

My aunts rally behind my baby sister – everyone adores her – and she grows up living with us.

While Mom is consumed with caring for Lilly and the household, Dad and I spend a lot of time doing things together. It's almost as if I am the son he never had. I help him with the yard work, planting azalea shrubs in the spring and raking leaves in the fall. I help him paint and plaster in the house and repair anything made of wood.

My father is a talented artist and I inherit some of his talent. I draw every day, even though Dad never says he likes my pictures and always corrects my perspective or technique. It's as if I'm possessed. Nothing can stop me from drawing. I come home from school and immediately set up my charcoal pencils and sketch pad on the dining room table. I sit for hours perfecting my creations, totally absorbed into a world where only my picture and I reside. And I always show my parents my latest drawing, usually of horses, but also portraits of famous people or people in our family – usually Dad or Liliana.

"Look at what I made!" I run to show Mom. I'm always a little in love with my latest picture.

Mom looks at it quickly, sideways, looking above it or around it. "Very nice dear," she says and goes back to whatever she's doing.

She doesn't seem to want me to draw. Drawing must feel dangerous to her. Is she afraid if she says she likes my drawing I will want to do more of it?

I get a sense she thinks the things I like to do are taking me away from the things I need to be doing in order to grow up properly. She's trying to guide me in the right direction, and I don't want to go there.

Dad will have already critiqued my picture as I was creating it and dismissed it as amateur work, so I don't have to show it to him. Cousins, aunts and uncles are always impressed by my pictures, but they aren't living at home with us and their praise doesn't make it any better when my parents aren't very interested in what I love to do.

Mom and Dad are much more interested in keeping me from doing things. Not only drawing, but everything. No sleepovers with friends. No stopping for pizza after school. Definitely no hanging out on a Saturday night. I am to come directly home after school. Weekends are for family. I don't learn much about social skills or being part of a group, but I must admit I don't miss it. To tell the truth, I am afraid of doing all those things with other kids. I don't fit in.

Still, life is good. I revel in the careless joy of childhood. I love our family, especially my sister and my cousins. I enjoy the summers, when I can be outside and play with my friends, or go on vacation with my parents and Liliana.

It's on our many vacations by the sea that my love of the ocean is born, with its explosions of Maine surf breaking against boulders, or miles of silver East Coast waves and spotted sandpipers with their legs speeding ahead of the whispering surf. I love falling asleep to the sounds of ocean surf and rattling sea grass. I love the cold smell of sand dunes and distant calls of seagulls in the morning. I write songs to the ocean and the sky and sing them as loud as I can at the water's edge where wind grabs the words as soon as they leave my lips and pulls them out to sea where they belong.

Yes, childhood is good. I am a loner by nature, and I don't mind living a quiet life within the family bubble.

Until.

The world changes. It's the mid 1960s. The Beatles come to America. Worse yet, the Rolling Stones come to America. Peace and Love are talked about. The Civil Rights Movement has created a new atmosphere that we don't speak about at home, but which I understand and feel. Boys start to grow long hair, and girl's hair gets even longer and windblown like a Joan Baez album cover. Beads are strung and worn around necks and ankles. Songs are sung about Maggie's Farm or times changing. My parents are not ready for times to change. But their daughter is a hippy and there isn't anything they can do about it.

I'm a strange kind of hippy. I love the beads, peace signs, tie-dye, and Indian sandals, but I'm not interested in drugs or alcohol. I understand I am not ready for sexual intimacy so even though I have a boyfriend, we never get beyond the petting stage. I am very clear about that and my boyfriend goes along with whatever I say. He truly loves me.

But my parents don't believe me when I explain I'm not interested in smoking pot or drinking. It's as if my parents don't know me. I am exactly the girl they raised, the rebellious girl who wants to do things, sing songs, write poems and draw pictures, but I absorbed and live all their values. I always want to be perfect for them, to finally do something right so they will love me.

I'm just too good to be real. Everything is backward in my life. My parents never believe I'm not drinking or using drugs. The funny thing is, I hate alcohol and never drink, but they don't believe me. It's obvious they don't know the signs of a drunken teenager. It's simple – they don't trust me. In all the years I live at home I am never trusted with a house key.

We only discuss the topic once, and my parents are a united front – I'm not getting a house key. Mom must think I will sneak out, but strangely enough that never crosses my mind.

Or she thinks I'll take advantage and try to sneak in after a night getting drunk and high. She's lying on the living room couch at 3 a.m. when I ring the bell after being out with my college friends. She jumps up to trap me at the door, frowning and smelling me, making me walk a straight line. It's crazy – my parents spend their life drumming values into me and then when I follow those values nobody believes I'm living them.

Mom starts to accuse me of having sex when I am around twelve years old. She wakes me up in the middle of the night shouting, "You're nothing but a street-walker! A trollop! Do you touch yourself?" She smacks at me in her frenzy, while I sit up in bed groggy from being awakened out of a deep sleep, protesting weakly and crying in shock. I have never heard these terms before, but I know they are related to sex. I'm not allowed to go anywhere, so how can I be a street-walker?

Dad stands behind her in the hallway moving his hands in a *slow down* motion. "Don't get her excited," he tells me. He is afraid Mom will turn her anger or fear or whatever it is on him, and he always agrees with anything she says when she is angry at me, especially if she has lost control. His denial hurt me more than anything Mom could ever say or do.

When I'm in high school we argue violently every night over the dinner table about drugs, which I'm not using. My teenage and young adult years are an alienating time. Long gone is the gut-burning helpless rage I felt as a young child when I couldn't control a situation. Now I cry every night, wracking sobs of frustration after every discussion with my parents. My eyes are constantly red and swollen. In the aftermath of each argument Mom brews strong tea and gives me the cold tea bags to put on my eyes so the swelling will go down. She hands them to me in a tired and resigned way, as if I'm a crazy person who needs something to calm her down.

I'm convinced that Mom and Dad are the crazy people.

By the age of sixteen I detach emotionally and become a sullen, angry, sarcastic kind of girl. It's the only way I can be alive and keep my sanity.

Is this when I abandoned myself? Does everyone go through this during the teenage years?

Sixteen becomes twenty-six. Pain becomes a form of narcissism and self-absorption. In my quest to do something that will make my parents happy, I decide to get married to the only guy I dated that they ever liked. But nobody explains to Liliana what my getting married means. How did we underestimate the depth of her feelings? Nobody tells her I'm not coming back home with her after the party. It's a cruel shock and I don't think she ever gets over it. From Liliana's point of view I abandoned her.

The reality of this memory is like beads of hot lead dripping into my brain. I hate this memory. I hate the stupidity and self-indulgence of it, of not thinking of my sister and her delicate feelings.

And as quickly as I think I hate this dark place, I leave it and go racing through the light. Slow down! Stop flying so fast. Find someone I love to pull me down to Earth from wherever I am. If I could find anyone, who would it be? Who taught me the most about how to love another being completely on their own terms?

Lil Tux.

After Liliana, the love of my life was not a man, or a woman, or even a child, but a cat. A feral, runty, black-and-white tuxedo cat. After Lilly, I can honestly say I love this cat more than anyone else I've ever known.

An animal. I've always been a Three Face after all.

CHAPTER TWELVE

I met her in the snow, during a cold spring in Upstate New York. I was living in my first apartment after officially ending my marriage to the wrong person. It was a small place facing onto the lawn behind the building. Each of the apartments in the rear had a small patio. The whole back area was bordered by thick shrubs and then woods beyond. On a day where a few blades of green grass were poking through the crust of old snow, I stepped out onto the patio – *my* patio – and finally felt right in the world. No more lies. Nobody there to step on my day. Me, the patio, and the snow. It was on this morning I first saw her, or rather, heard her. She was hiding in the shrubs rimming the lawn and meowing tentatively at me.

Her voice said "I'm starving and desperate and frightened to ask a human for help." She had to show herself so, green eyes very big and whiskers forward, she crept toward me as I swept the patio of snow and crumbled leaves, searching for traces of life in the salt-stained clay pots standing in a row on my patio. I watched without looking directly at her, then stopped sweeping and quietly went into the apartment for some food. I kept a few cans of cat food thinking someday a stray might find its way to me. And here she was. I put a dish of food on the edge of the patio and backed away. She ate every bit without taking her stricken green eyes off me.

Every day she came to my patio. She was young and charming and seemed very intelligent. Her back legs were long like a rabbit's and her tail was shorter than I thought it should be. At first she came with a male cat that looked a lot like her, only large and very sleek. He must have been a litter mate. She was starting to trust me, and tried to share food with her friend to help him survive. He came around a few times, then disappeared. And then there was only Lil Tux. That's what I named her for her white muzzle, chest and paws and small stature.

When spring turned to summer, Tux began to nose around the patio entrance of my apartment, staring inside with one paw up and nostrils wide open. It was a miracle she survived the freezing winter with three feet of snow on the ground. Her jaws were very small and although she was athletic, I could see she didn't have much luck as a hunter. Perhaps her beautiful soul was too gentle for her to kill things and eat them. Whatever the case, Tux made up her mind to trust me and finally let me pet her.

From there it wasn't long before she came regularly into the apartment. Her black fur shone as she lay on the rug in a patch of sunlight, her belly pure spotless white. She lay on her back with her front legs reaching over her head and her back toes reaching out behind her, luxuriating in the safety. No raccoons. No mean cats with big teeth. No skunks or coyotes. When she was inside she looked like she had found heaven. She became affectionate and almost too demanding when she wanted attention. I wasn't sure I wanted to be ruled by a cat but there was a magic about her that made me keep feeding and helping her.

In the 1980s nobody had heard of Trap-Neuter-Release. Inevitably Lil Tux became pregnant, though she seemed so young and small. Soon she was like a barrel and her time to deliver was near. She began placing mouthfuls of fur under an old high-legged Victrola stand that sat in my living room corner. Before I knew it, a soft cushion of white belly fur lay over the carpet in an exact square under the stand. But instead of having the kittens in my apartment she tried to go it alone like a true feral mother. One morning she turned up looking slim once more, and frantic. She disappeared after grabbing a mouthful of food and in a short while appeared again at the patio door with a kitten dangling from her jaws. When I opened the door she trotted with head held high to the nest she had created and deposited a fat grey bundle. She brought no more kittens. I imagined her newborn brood had been attacked in the night, and she, such a timid girl, had been unable to defend them. During the day she nursed and cleaned the one grey kitten that I named Angel, but each night she yowled to be let out. When I opened the patio door she melted into the night and was gone for hours. I called and called, confused by her disappearance, and eventually she would come back looking frazzled and wild.

After about two weeks of this routine Angel was getting fat and Tux remained frantic, especially when evening approached. Angel was a very placid kitten though he was starting to be curious about the rest of the apartment. Lil Tux continued her disappearing act every evening. One morning after disappearing overnight she appeared at the patio door with another kitten in her mouth, a skinny grey and white female, twisting and hissing. Now I understood. Tux had been nurturing this other kitten in the original nest and hadn't been brave enough to move her until now. I named this smaller kitten Baby.

Baby was about half the size of Angel and not complacent at all. She was feisty and peed all over everything in my apartment. A trip to the vet revealed that she had Guardia, ear mites and worms. A lot of medication went into her pint-sized body to help her get well, and to hopefully improve her attitude!

Eventually both kittens were adopted. Lil Tux promptly began to swell up again with a new litter of kittens. She had two other litters, and I managed to get all the kittens adopted with the help of my next-door neighbor Janie and various friends.

At around this time, I decided it was time to move. I was working in New York City and my commute was nearly three hours each way. I hoped Lil Tux would decide to move along with me. I hated the thought of leaving her behind.

She tried, she really tried, following me out to the car and putting her paws up to look inside as I loaded it up with belongings destined for my new place. But she couldn't get up the courage to get into the car. As my furniture moved and the apartment emptied she started hanging out by my next door neighbor Janie's patio. She had lost some of the bounce in her gait, but she accepted Janie's petting and food. She didn't want to leave the yard where she was born. It was her whole world.

I moved, and kept in touch with Janie so I could keep tabs on Lil Tux. I worried constantly about her. Would Janie understand her as I did? Would she take care of her every day? Again Tux became pregnant and Janie and I talked about what we should do. This couldn't go on.

Janie called me late one night. Lil Tux had begun delivering the latest litter of kittens in her living room. I hopped in the car and got over there as fast as I could. Lil Tux was doing well, but then things stopped. She strained, then gave up when nothing happened. She strained again, and nothing happened. Her stomach was roiling with kittens, but nothing else came out. We panicked and called the Emergency Vet Service. Working with them over the phone was getting us nowhere and we were instructed to bring Tux in so they could assist in the delivery of the rest of her kittens. I gently tried to lift her into a cat carrier, but she was ungainly with all the kittens moving around inside and I couldn't get a good hold on her. The movement of her body as I handled her seemed to shift the unborn kittens into new positions, and she began delivering again! When it was all done she had delivered seven kittens. My God. How were we going to find homes for this group? Something had to change.

At about this time the local feral queen cat attacked Lil Tux. The queen was getting old and must have had FIV from living her hard life. Lil Tux's nose was scratched in the scuffle, after which she began to show signs of having been infected with feline leukemia, developing what seemed like a mild cold. The scratch on her nose never truly healed all the way. This was the last straw. I decided to adopt Lil Tux and make her an indoor cat to keep her safe.

I packed her off one night in a cat carrier and brought her to my new apartment. Tux was completely traumatized. Being put into a box and then into an unfamiliar bigger box is a feral cat's idea of death. She crept out of the carrier and smashed herself into a far corner of my bedroom, behind the bed, staying there for about five days. Hunger drove her from her hiding place a few times, but after eating she crawled back under the bed. She wouldn't look at me. She hated the litter pan. She wanted her own yard. Once she decided to come out of hiding she sat on the windowsill for hours staring into the woods at the edge of my new back yard.

I did not want her going outside. The woods may have seemed safe to her but I knew they were filled with raccoons, foxes and coyotes and she didn't know the territory. But one night after she'd been at my apartment for around three weeks, Lil Tux made her move. She streaked through the door when I stepped out to throw away the garbage, and in one swift movement I had lost her!

"Tux! Come back!" Her small blackness melted into the dusk as she bolted for the garden. I could hear her moving through the undergrowth as she began to explore the woods beyond. She ignored my calls. I walked out toward the woods, which drove her further away.

She had been outside for an hour or so, during which time dusk had turned into night and with it, screams, snarls and crashing noises came from the woods as animals careened in the dark. It had to be Lil Tux getting into trouble with another cat or a wild animal that could kill her.

I ran out into the yard and frantically called to her. "Tux, come on, come up here now!" I ran into the woods clapping my hands and yelling to break up the fight. The screaming and sounds of struggle stopped, but no Tux appeared. I went back to my door and sat on the stoop for what seemed like hours. Every so often I softly called her name, but stayed by the doorway so I wouldn't scare her back into the woods. If Tux was alive, she could see me and would find her way back. Soon it was pitch black and dead quiet in the yard. Crunching in the woods told me something was walking in the undergrowth. A shadow with a white chest and face appeared at the edge of the garden.

"Tux," I whispered. "Come on Tux." She bolted across the expanse of lawn, I opened the door and she flashed inside.

She stank of an acrid animal smell and there was a small gash on her left flank. She was limping, triumphant and excited, but I was frightened. If she had been another cat I would have packed her off to the vet, but Tux had just recovered from being moved in the cat carrier.

I cleaned her fur with a damp cloth and dabbed at the gash with soap and water. She struggled against me, but I wrapped her in a towel to gain control and keep from getting clawed. I put some antibiotic cream on the gash; she promptly twisted away from me and maniacally licked the cream off the wound.

Later that night Tux quieted down, a bit too much. I felt her ears and paws. She seemed hot to the touch. The gash on her leg was bright red. Afraid of infection, I doused the wound with peroxide and pushed more antibiotic cream into the opening.

I sat up with her all night, stroking her while she purred and looked up at me with her trusting green eyes. By the next morning she seemed to have an appetite, but I didn't like the look of the gash. I contacted the local vet and coaxed them into giving me some antibiotic pills, and after around ten days on the medication Tux seemed to be healing. She mostly lost her taste for the great outdoors, but occasionally ran through the open door and poked around outside for a short while. She was always back within the hour, standing at the edge of the garden until she could see me at the door, then streaking across the lawn and back into the safety of our apartment.

Once Tux got used to being inside we had some happy years. She was the perfect house cat. She didn't jump on the furniture and didn't claw anything but an old worm-eaten stump I brought into the house as a scratching post. We played tag and hide and seek. Her language was a constant expressive repertoire of meows and chirps. She knew my routine and got used to my friends. I never expected to love her as much as I did.

Then I took her to the vet for a teeth cleaning and when she came home something was wrong. As she walked around the house she would stretch her right leg out behind her, looking up at me and meowing. At first I thought it was some new way she had devised of being playful, but soon I could see the leg twitch slightly every minute or so. It got worse every day and soon the leg twitched every few seconds, day and night. I took her to the vet but he had no answers. Drugs didn't help, they made her groggy. Tux turned off the twitching leg as much as possible so the twitch could be tolerated, and the leg became dead and useless. Initially she was able to hobble to the litter pan and around the house dragging the leg along, and then she couldn't walk anymore. The spinal column was affected. Eventually she needed help to eat; I had to hold her body with my hands on either side of her face and neck to keep her esophagus straight for each swallow of food. The vet said it was a neurological issue affecting her whole system. Perhaps she had had a stroke. I tried everything I could think of to help her and keep her alive, but it was all trial and error. Since she couldn't make it on her own to the litter box I tried using diapers during the day when I went to work, but she pulled them off. She'd be in a different spot in the apartment every night when I got home depending on how she'd flopped around during the day. I'd whistle for her when I came in and she'd meow back so I could find her.

Perhaps I shouldn't have tried to tame her. She was, after all, a wild animal. Maybe she was meant to live out her life in the rhythms of light and dark, cold and wet, hot and frigid, only needing my assistance now and then to live in joy and freedom. If I had left her wild she wouldn't have gotten the twitch at all. Or maybe she would have become ill and died alone in misery and pain. I'll never know. But she lived with me and the twitch came, and got worse, and we lived on together. I should have bathed her to remove the urine from her fur from the times she couldn't make it to the litter pan but Tux hated the water and when I tried bathing her she flopped away from me growling and spitting. Stinking and with certain parts broken and other parts strangely intact, she lived on with a dignity only a wild animal can muster.

I helped her eat, I helped her poop and pee, and I sang to her while she purred. Eyes clear and cognizant, she tried her best, devising different chirps to tell me when she was hungry or when she had to be carried to the litter. One night I heard something in my sleep. Lil Tux! Her name sounded loud and clear and woke me up. I sat upright in bed with my eyes wide open, adjusting to the darkness.

"Lil Tux! Oh my God! I'm here, I'm right here!"

I ran over to her sleeping place by the bedroom door, a few steps from the bed. She had gotten smothered under her favorite woolen blanket. She seemed torpid, not moving, limp and very hot. Was she dead!? I was certain her soul floated above me as I sat holding her fevered body for hours in the dark room, but then why did she not grow cold? I leaned my face down to hers to see if I could feel breath. Tears streamed from my eyes for all those hours as I held a limp, warm cat in my hands. Then around dawn, she took in a huge breath and stirred. She began to breathe regularly and purr deeply. I believe most of her lives slipped out of her that night, but at least one life slipped back in and by morning she was alive and I was so grateful to have my friend back, even if she was stinky and twitching.

Sometimes I lost patience, especially on week days when I had to feed her and get her to use the litter while rushing to get ready for work. She would pull herself up onto the bed sometimes so I could put my hand on the twitching limb. All night I would lie awake trying to keep my hand on her so the weight could hold the twitch still, ease her pain and let her sleep. I tried massage but it hurt her and she would hiss and growl. I knew she wasn't ready to give up, so I continued with her in her wretched state. Like a true wild being, she held onto life with claws and teeth. Friends who visited didn't say anything but I could see by their faces how appalled they were that I kept her alive like this. I knew she wasn't ready for death. Her instincts were to keep on going until she dropped, and I was determined to help.

One morning, she wasn't able to poop. She strained. I supported her hind legs. She pushed but nothing happened. We tried for a long while until she became exhausted. I knew the time had come to let this small, beautiful, urine-soaked, broken being go from this life. We weren't ready, but I put her in the cat carrier. She was terrified and so was I.

A friend whose cats I minded when she traveled had recommended a local vet. She said he was kind. We drove there, and were led into a sterile room with a stainless-steel table and a chair.

The vet came into the room and with no fanfare or explanation, he gave her a shot.

He wasn't kind! He wasn't gentle! He jabbed the needle into her hind quarters and she cried out! Her last words were a cry! I'll never forget that horror. I was furious at the vet, but the deed was done and now it was my time to sit with her as she took her last breaths on Earth. The shot immobilized her, but her green eyes remained wide open, unblinking and staring. I held her as she breathed. Her heart skipped a few beats but it was strong. I held her and talked to her. The vet stood there with me for a short while, still saying nothing, then he walked out of the room. I was determined to stay with her until she died so she wouldn't be afraid. She took deep rasping breaths and I waited, holding her like a beautifully wrapped package with her paws tucked neatly under her chest and her tail neatly curved forward around her haunches. Slowly I realized the vet would not give her the killing shot while I was in the room, though he had never explained the process. I walked quietly out, turning around with each step to see her, unmoving and compact on the steel table, green eyes open, still breathing. Did you see me Lil Tux?

"Yes Mommy, I saw you."

Yikes! What was that voice?

I'm crying and floating above a vast field of grass far below me, iridescent like no grass I have ever seen. I drop down slowly as though sinking into a deep green pillow. The air around me is soft like feathers on my skin.

"Looking through my eyes was hazy," the voice continues. "I saw you crying and I didn't want to see that anymore. I was glad when the man finally stuck me with a needle and made the twitch stop once and for all. At first I was afraid, but when I understood you were helping to end the pain, I was glad.

"Did you see me after you went home? I saw you cry and then get angry when you threw out all my dishes, and the litter pan, and the placemat where you fed me. You cried when you put my blanket in the laundry. I didn't want you to be so sad, so I came back to see you every day. I know you saw me."

"Tux? Is that you? It sounds like you." How would I know? I never heard her speak.

"Yes, it's me. I heard you calling, and now I found you. Did you see me after I left?"

She heard me calling? She speaks? She sees me?

Just go with it.

"I saw a shadow like you. Was it you all those times? When you first left I saw the shadow walking near my legs a lot. I heard your cute voice sometimes when no one was there but me. I've never stopped seeing you. Even now, sometimes I think I see your shiny darkness moving between my other cats. I call my cat Chloe by your name sometimes. Every so often I think you are alive again in her."

"Sometimes I am. Mostly I'm here though, and I come to see you when I get lonely. I try to get close enough for you to pet me but I can't feel anything. I don't think you can feel me either."

"You're right, I can't. Maybe now we can. I'm here now, wherever here is."

I'm surprised and wondering how things have instantly changed. How is all this happening? All I did was think of Lil Tux, and now she's here.

I reach out my hand to stroke her glossy fur. It's smooth and very warm from the sun. I get on my knees and put my cheek on hers. Yes, she's fur and cat breath again. Like she's alive! She *is* alive! My Lil Tux!

I'm getting excited now. This place has possibilities. "I'm so glad I'm able to come here so we can be together again! Will you take me to your favorite spots soon? Like you did when we lived Upstate, where we first met?"

"I'll lead you as I did back then. Remember how I ran ahead and turned back to wait for you to catch up? We climbed up to my special rock, where I looked down on the building, the parking lot, my whole world. I basked on my rock in the daytime, and waited to see your car come home. Even if it was late and dark, I knew when you arrived and I'd call to you. *Mommy, I'm hungry!* And you'd answer from the parking lot, calling up into the woods, *OK Lil Tux, come around back and we'll eat!*

"I always wondered how you knew when I came home."

"I could see the light in the bedroom too. Remember when I came to the window and called you? I knew both sides of the building, and I knew which windows were yours."

"You were very smart! The smartest cat I ever knew! I'm so proud of you!"

"Thanks! But that was a long time ago in another life. Let's play now! I'll lead you over to the soft grass. I have some friends to show you.

CHAPTER THIRTEEN

Lil Tux bounds ahead of me through neon green grass and fragrant Queen Anne's lace as tall as my head. We seem to be running toward the edge of a woods. I am somehow able to keep up. My body has no limits.

Long before we reach the trees I see a large rusty brown blur moving back and forth through the grass. The blur is not distinct because it's moving at blinding speed. I zero in on who or what it is.

My eyes work differently here and anything I think of comes instantly into focus. I concentrate on the blur and it slows down almost to stillness while the limbs keep moving in minute increments and the wavy fur flops in slow motion with each stride.

It's a big dog. Now that he's slowed down every detail is visible. Yellow eyes, red tongue lolling out the side of his mouth, and very white teeth when he smiles. He bounds up to Tux, who jumps back and forth over his head using her long back legs like springs. His joyful voice fills the air. Could it be Boozer? He's shouting excitedly to Tux now.

"I love running so much! It's my favorite thing! I'm glad I finally figured out I'm a dog! Hey Tux, I bet you can't catch me! Wow, that sun feels so warm! I have an idea. Let's go to the beach and dig in the sand! I remember I used to go to the beach with the girl I loved more than anyone else I ever knew. The farm where I lived after living with her was very exciting, with all the horses and cows and the three boys. I even liked the chickens! They were so much fun to chase. I loved my new masters too. But I never forgot the girl. She was my first human. I really, *really* miss her!"

"I've brought you someone," says Lil Tux in between high jumps and athletic flips over Boozer's head.

The big, rusty-colored dog looks up with a mouth full of green grass to see me, not the girl he remembers, and stops dead in his tracks. I must look like a stranger now. I'm much older and probably taller, not skinny and tan but pale and thick in the middle. He looks the same with his reddish-brown curls, unruly eyebrows and whiskers, yellow eyes and short tail. Large and very substantial. My dog! My beautiful Boozer!

Lil Tux steps to one side of me. I feel scared. How will this dog feel about me? I was too young to know how to train him properly, and my parents didn't know how to train him either, even though they should have known something, shouldn't they? He was always so wild. He chewed up everything in sight, especially anything made of wood like the living room furniture and kitchen cabinets. Dad blamed his wildness on me. I tried my best but at age thirteen and having no experience working with dogs, I didn't have much chance of training him or understanding why he was so hyper. He was my first pet and it would have been good for me to get some guidance from a responsible adult. Too bad there were none around.

We made a lot of mistakes. In today's pet-enlightened world we would be called poor dog owners. For starters, we didn't neuter him or let him run in a field to burn up all his energy. And we should have waited until he was three or four months old before taking him away from his dog mother to begin with. Instead, we adopted him at two weeks old and he imprinted on me. I don't think he ever understood he was a dog and not a human.

"Boozer! It's me!" I am so excited I can barely contain it. I start jumping up and down as though I'm still the thirteen-year-old girl who loved her dog more than anything else in the world, except for her sister of course.

He has stopped running and looks me up and down, sniffing the air. With lowered head he takes a few steps toward me.

"Boozer," I say simply, so he can hear my voice. I don't think my voice has changed as much as the rest of me.

His shaggy muzzle explodes into a smile and he runs the rest of the way. He crashes into me and we fall, laughing and tumbling in the electric green grass under the waving branches of giant Queen Anne's lace. Even though he has barreled into me at full solid speed and knocked me off my feet, nothing hurts. We're rolling around laughing together! I love this place!

"I can't believe it's you!" Boozer dances and licks and waggles and smiles as only a big joyful dog can do.

I throw my arms around his neck and rub my tears into his coarse fur. "Boozer, I'm so sorry we gave you away." I find it hard to speak. "Mom and Dad, they didn't know how to take care of you. I was just a kid. I didn't have anything to say about it."

"I know. I know it wasn't your idea. I was a pretty lucky dog. I got to live with you when I was young, and then you gave me to a shelter where they train all of us animals and decide what we'd be good at so we can have another chance to find the right life. It was a nice place. When I got there, they showed me things dogs are supposed to do, like walking on a leash without pulling, and not chewing on furniture and shoes.

"For so long I thought I was your brother or son. I didn't know how to be a dog and I didn't *want* to be a dog. I don't remember my mother. I remember the girl who carried me home in her arms. You gave me a blanket, a stuffed toy dog to cuddle with, and your own soft sweater in a shoebox for my bed. Then when everyone else was asleep you snuck downstairs and lay next to me all night so I wouldn't be frightened in my new home. I remember how you sat with me smoothing my fur, how you made me oatmeal to eat because I was so young and barely had any teeth. You sang to me, took me for walks, protected me from bigger dogs and mean kids when I was a pup. We ran on the beach chasing sea gulls when I got bigger. You taught me hand signals, how to Stay, and how to Shake Hands. *What's up there,* you'd ask, pointing to the ceiling. *Rouf, rouf, rouf,* I'd bark as loud as I could. You thought I was so smart.

"I slept with you on the bed when I got bigger. I thought I was human. The first time I saw myself in a mirror I was pretty shocked. *What is that ugly, hairy thing,* I thought. I believed I should look like you, sleek with smooth skin and long brown hair on my head. At least the hair color was similar, even if mine wasn't long like yours."

"Well, I don't look that way anymore," I say. I feel like crying for everything that was. Those were precious moments in my young life, lived long ago and so briefly, after dreaming I could have a dog of my own instead of playing with the neighbor's dog, or my cousin's dog, or a stranger's dog.

He looks me up and down again. He walks all around me and smells my legs and my hands. He jumps up, puts his paws on my shoulders, and smiles. "You still look the same to me," he says, sticks his big brown nose into my cheek and licks my face. Dog kisses! The best!

I'm so glad my Boozer had a good life. Relieved. Absolved. "What did you do on the farm?" I ask.

"It was a small farm and they had three kids, all boys. The boys and I ran through the woods and played fetch by a brook. I kept them safe. Nobody challenged me. I watched over those stupid chickens and the house too. They had two other dogs, Boomer and Clyde, so I had friends. They changed my name to Rusty. I was a dog, and I liked it. But tell me – how's Lilly?"

Of course, he remembers my baby sister, Liliana. Boozer adored my sister. Being half German Shepard and half Standard Poodle he was super smart and protective. He guarded Lilly and made sure she didn't run into the street when she was playing in the yard. Nobody could make a threatening gesture toward her. *Nobody.* Not even Dad. If they seemed to threaten her or even get too near, Boozer would growl and get ready to attack. Of course, I would never make a threatening gesture toward her. I always loved her too much. And anyway, Boozer was my dog. I know he'd never attack me.

"Boozer?"

He's run off chasing something. I think it's the wind. This is a place where you can chase the wind because you can see it.

Liliana. Who has a sister they love more than their own life? Who has someone they can always love and who will love them forever? I do.

My sister was born with Down Syndrome. Long ago when she was born the doctors were very ignorant, even more than they are now. They called her names like Mentally Retarded, and Mongoloid. They gave my parents no hope, like having my sister was the end of their lives.

We depended on the doctors for information, and Liliana's disability was delivered to us as devastating news. My Dad never accepted that my imperfect sister had happened to our family. He had been so happy with a nice house, a job in art he loved, a beautiful wife and a little girl – but now an imperfect child. A Mongoloid. She would never be able to do anything or be anything. That's what the doctors told him.

Put her in a home Frank, they told him. *It's the best thing.*

Thankfully my parents decided to keep her at home. She was part of our family.

Retarded, Mongoloid, Down Syndrome, slow, stupid. But my sister is so much more than those names, those ideas. She has an innate knowledge of God. A direct line. I've always known it.

This place is new to me. I don't know how it works when I want to see people on Earth. I've seen Lil Tux and my dog, Boozer, but they are here like I am. I haven't tried to see anyone who is still living.

I think I should look for Liliana.

My beautiful sister is now a 58-year-old person living in a group home for mentally challenged people. I wonder how she's reacted to my sudden disappearance from her life. Has anyone told her I'm dead? If they haven't she must wonder why she hasn't seen me for, well, how long has it been? I have no idea!

Or is everyone going to pretend she doesn't know the difference, and she won't notice I'm gone?

Lilly understands death. She has lost nearly everyone she loves. But she doesn't have to lose me. I can find her.

I start to work on it. I start to think about Lilly. In this place, whatever I think about comes to me.

I have a sudden sensation of falling, and I claw at thick air so I won't go down so fast. While I slip down I try to see where Lilly is.

"Liliana. Lilly." Then louder. "Lilly!" I see her, I'm above her now. Yes, she's looking. She's not interested yet. She's playing with her CDs in the living room at the group home where she lives, picking them up, switching the jewel cases, shoving them into one of her tote bags, and carrying them to the cabinet where she keeps her favorite ones.

"Lilly. It's Evie." That gets her attention. She looks up and around.

Now she's talking. "Evie," she says quietly, mostly to herself.

"It's me. I wanted to say Hi. I'm in a new place. So far, I've seen Boozer, and Uncle Larrson and Aunt Toni."

Very slowly, she puts down her CDs and sits back quietly, looking around and listening. She looks good. Her dark hair is salt and pepper now, like Dad's, and the color suits her. She looks clean and healthy the way she looked the last time I saw her. I hope it hasn't been too long. I'm thinking I could have visited her more often when I was there, though we did a lot together. We traveled to see relatives, I took her to physical therapy to keep her strong, stopped for ice cream at Carvel, went shopping for clothes and more CDs, ate at IHop, and did lots of sleepovers. We talked, a lot! I was always there when she needed something. But when you love someone so much it's never enough.

Well, she hears me now. She hears me but can't see me. It must be confusing for her. And very slowly, she starts to cry. Crystal tears roll down her cheeks. She looks around her to see where the voice is coming from. She doesn't understand. How could she?

This was a bad idea! Who was it for? I thought when we die we become better. Was this idea to come see her from some place of Ego? Always Ego, always about myself, ruining every moment. If seeing and hearing me makes her cry then we are not doing it!

But how incredible! She heard me!

"Okay, my love. Don't cry, my angel. I came to tell you I will always love you through time and space. Forever."

"Evie. Evie." She's still crying but not as much. She gets up from where she's sitting and walks into the next room to tell the aids she's heard from Evie. They won't understand what she's saying, but they will soothe her and let her know everything is okay.

Now I'm crying too, because she will continue to live in that house away from the family. Mom and Dad and all the Aunts have long since passed away. The visits from cousins will get further and further apart. At least Paul will check in on her and take care of any issues, but I know I will never speak to her again.

CHAPTER FOURTEEN

Well, that was awful. How could I be so stupid? I need to think before I act. Even here, mistakes can be made. Our mistakes cost people on Earth something. The dead can reach us though we think we've lost them. Be careful. The dead have power for good, and for ill.

No more playing with human feelings. It doesn't matter how much I want to see them or tell them I'm okay. But what about my cats? They must be able to handle a short visit without being afraid or sad to hear from me.

I want to find Olive. He's a small gray cat but he's big inside. I remember the first time I saw him, a small kitten in a cage full of bigger kittens. His face looked up, and a pink mouth opened in a silent meow.

He was the runt, so naturally I adopted him. Because he was so small I kept him apart from my other cats at first. He lived in the bedroom and I took care of his every need. Food. Litter. Stomach upsets. Broken paws. Playing. Hugging. His miniature frame fit neatly under my chin. He would climb up my chest and lay there looking up at me, purring loudly. So here was yet another creature who imprinted on me. Olive, where are you now? Mommy didn't mean to leave you.

Much as I want to see Olive, I don't want to frighten him. I feel certain he will see or feel me. I always believed that would be possible with animals. It was true with Lil Tux, when she came back to Earth for visits, but I never saw her clearly; she was a shadowy suggestion of herself, disappearing when I tried to get a better look. I heard her much more clearly than I ever saw her after she left. The good thing is it wasn't frightening. I don't want to frighten anyone any more than I already have. Can I make clear contact with an animal? I'm going to try with Olive.

I already made my way down through the thickness covering Liliana. Please, let me see my apartment once more. I flow like I'm doing the sidestroke through time. Stroke, stroke. When was the last time I did this? It's familiar.

Oh. Yes. Astara stroked through the killing tides so she could wash up on a pebble shore and live another day. Are we all doomed to repeat the same actions again and again, no matter what our form?

"Olive." If I say his name a few times we might be able to make contact. "Olive. Olive." Breathing, stroking my arms through invisible water.

"Mommy! Where are you? I need you! I hear you but I can't see you. Can you come and play now? I miss you! Hurry Moose – Mommy is here!" His is a sweet, high-pitched kind of whiney voice.

"Wait Olive, wait small boy. You know I'm dead, right? You found me. You know I'll never come back to play." That sounds so final. Reality hits me and I am deeply sad, robbed, and heavy.

"Dead? What's dead? I know you didn't move, and then Daddy found you and he rushed around and cried, and people took you away. When can you come back? Daddy brushes us and he is giving us our favorite food, but he doesn't play run and hide behind the bedroom door like you do."

"I am here now but I can't do much better than this. Dead means I went someplace far away and I'm not coming back."

I can see his piercing yellow eyes and cute gray lips looking surprised and hurt. A lot of hurt. I should *not* have tried this. Another failed experiment. Everything I have to say is painful. What's the good of hurting everyone I love? It's not making me or them feel better when I come back.

Olive is running through the apartment in circles, making a circuit under the chair legs, over the coffee table, rebounding off the wall and bouncing into the bedroom. He meows frantically as he runs back and forth now in the hallway.

"Calm down now. Is Daddy playing with you? Is Moose being nice? Are you and Chloe getting along?"

"Daddy plays our favorite string game with us. He tries very hard. I love him very much, but not as much as you Mommy. Chloe misses you. She looks out the window all day expecting you to come down the walk. Moose is grumpy. He pooped under your chair a few times since you left. Daddy plays the song you made up for him on the guitar to cheer him up, and tells us you will come back soon."

"I can't come back." He's jumping all over the apartment now. He's on the bookcase yowling. That's his playful call.

"Come down off the bookcase now, Olive." He leaps gracefully from the bookcase across half the room and back into the hallway. "You're such a good boy!"

"Will you visit me again though? Please? I miss your smell. The bed feels empty. Daddy talks to us like you could be back home any day. When can you come home?"

"I'll visit again. Tell Moose and Chloe I miss them and love them very much. Tell Daddy too, even if he doesn't understand."

"Okay Mommy."

"Olive?"

"Yes?"

"Do cats love people?"

"Yes, of course! They love people more than people love people!"

"Good. I'm glad. Now be a good boy. Bye."

✦

What did he mean, Daddy talks like I could be back any day? It doesn't make any sense.

I'm back in the grass and it's a blessing, so fresh and moist and alive. It may be the only living thing here. I guess I'm technically dead. Technically.

I am beginning to understand. Flat brain waves, heart on assistance, beeps. I hear them now, through the mist. I thought my body died, but I was wrong.

Uncle Larrson and Aunt Toni will explain all this to me if I can find them again.

I think I see something. A shape, getting larger and sharper. A person. It's going to take me a while to figure out how this works.

"Uncle Larrson, is that you again?"

"I see you're finding your way around."

I can see him better now. He looks good out here in the green field. The same steely hair in the military cut and steely blue eyes crinkling with his smile. He's tall, not bent over with speckled bony hands like he was after the stroke.

Now there's an interesting question. What do I look like now? I haven't seen any mirrors around here, and it's probably better that way. There is so much to see outside of myself I haven't been very concerned with seeing my own image. I look at my hands. Do they look smoother?

"Uncle Larrson, I'm still trying to find out how things work around here. I've been doing some traveling back to Earth, but I'm not sure if it's the right thing to do. You know, trying to talk to people, to show myself."

"Personally, I think it's better to act behind the scenes. People miss those they can't see or talk to anymore, and I think it's best not to open wounds. Let them heal."

"You're saying I shouldn't try to communicate?"

"Not directly. You see, you can be watching and helping without them knowing. It's kinder that way, to make it seem like we are totally separated. Much less stressful I'd say."

"Where's Aunt Toni? Still spending time with her Papa?"

"Yes. She spends a lot of time with Mama, Chris and Alex too."

Papa, Mama, Alex. Aunt Toni lost her father and brothers when they were all young. It makes sense she'd make up for lost time with all of them now.

"I should make time to visit the people in my family I never met," I say. Or think. Larrson answers, so I guess thinking and speaking are the same thing here.

"Don't bother, there are too many. Concentrate on a few, the most important ones."

"I don't know. Anyway, how do you watch over the people you love?"

"Well, you already know the answer to that question. You always thanked your Guardians, the souls hovering over you, as well as God, Jesus, all the Saints and the Angels. You know about Guardians. 'Guardian Angel' is the popular term used on Earth, if I remember correctly. We're no Angels, but I've been able to stop any number of car accidents, for example. I've kept you safe many times, and you thanked me each time. Though of course I don't do it alone."

"Who else helps?"

"Your Mom and Dad of course. They watched over you in life so you must know they watch over you still."

"Yes. Well. I'll think about that. I mean, I'll think about whether I want to see them."

"I think you should. I think you will."

A stubborn, stuck feeling grabs me in my gut. I don't need to see Mom and Dad. What would it accomplish? In those decisive moments of life, you want to go to your parents because you're lost and desperate and frightened. I never went to my parents. I thought I knew that instead of help there would be judgment and retribution, instead of patience and wisdom to help me get back on track there would be a critique of my life and my actions, and the punishment that I would have to take care of things myself. Like every other time when I needed help or guidance, all they had for me was a lecture about how selfish I am, how foolish. No, I can't see them.

But there is someone I would like to see. My vanity kicks in. "Uncle Larrson, what do I look like?"

"Why, you're as lovely and smart as the last time I saw you!"

I should have known. "I'll see you again soon. Tell Aunt Toni hello for me."

"OK, honey."

Dispersing in a rush of clipped grey, he is gone and I am alone with some decisions to make.

CHAPTER FIFTEEN

The truth must be told. I didn't live a perfect life. I did things I regret. Mom and Dad – and The Old One – were right about me.

I was selfish. I was foolish. We don't say the word *wrong* here but we do say *regret*. I know the actions of my life can't be corrected or erased. They stand for all time. They are recorded somewhere. I don't want to think about that now.

I made mistakes and did things I shouldn't have done but most of those things were minor infractions, lapses in judgment, egotistical errors. They didn't impact other people, only me. I wasn't faced with many important life choices, but one in particular is haunting me now as it never did before.

I thought my choice was right. It *seemed* like the only choice I could make at the time. It was a frantic choice to save my own life – or sanity – because I felt so hopeless and without possibilities. I'm talking about a women's unique choice. I'm talking about abortion.

Was I a morally bankrupt person who forgot the difference between right and wrong? When did I lose my self-respect? I tried to stay married and I always thought I wanted to have a family. That was certainly what my parents wanted.

I wasn't married for very long before I had to accept the fact I had made a huge error in judgment in my choice of husband. But I was married long enough to feel pressure from all sides to start a family. From the first day of my marriage I knew I was on shaky ground, but I so much wanted it to work. I tried every day, but I didn't know how to set the marriage right.

Back then I thought I was the only one who ever made the mistake of marrying the wrong person, probably for the wrong reasons. Now I wonder if many people don't also make this mistake.

Soon after getting married, I was laid off from my job. My husband Russell made a very good living selling life insurance in New York City, so my meager earnings from a State-sponsored job in the criminal court system weren't missed. After working at regular sales or office jobs, I wanted to do something that would make a difference in people's lives. I landed a position as criminal court screener for a program called the Second Chance Project. This program suspended criminal court cases for nine months mainly for youth who were starting to get embroiled in a life of crime, to show them another way. Through the program they could get a job, or get training, or go back to school; they were shown that alternatives to stealing exist.

There were rules. No violent crime, no weapons charges. No person in the program could get arrested while they were participating in the program, or their case was placed back into the normal court process. Most participants managed to stay out of trouble.

They had to meet with program counselors each week, who kept them on track and made home visits to understand the environment a participant came from. Our counselors were seasoned men who had been through one system or another themselves – or all the systems – so they had credibility. They already knew every scam because they'd lived them.

The program worked. The people we accepted into the program weren't hardened criminals, they were mainly youth arrested for non-violent crimes. Some were beyond our help. If drugs were involved we referred the person to another unit run by the court system. We tried working with young prostitutes – our hearts genuinely went out to these girls – but we quickly learned if you got them into the program they'd walk out of jail saying yes to anything, and you'd never see them again. They lied about everything, you never even knew their real names. It was all part of the life.

Times were tough in those days for men in their fifties who had lost their jobs, as it is now. Sometimes we took a man into the program who had been arrested for an offense such as stealing points and spark plugs so he could do car tune-ups for cash. Usually these middle-aged men had never been arrested before, and they were mortified that their families would find out. We located jobs for them and they earned adjournments of their court cases that led to dismissal, provided they did not get arrested again for the prescribed period of time.

But most of the participants were young, poor and poorly educated, and were getting involved in theft and other misdemeanors because they didn't know another way to survive. We helped a lot of people leave the court and prison system before they ever got into it. Our recidivist arrest record was excellent; hardly any of our participants were arrested again in the two years I worked for the program.

The cops on the beat got to know us and went from resenting a bunch of arrogant college kids to appreciating the work we were doing because they saw it could work. Many of them let us know when they arrested someone who could benefit from our program. Everyone knew the court system is a revolving door, but until our program arrived there was no way to change things. The police wanted change like everyone else did. Our program was an instrument of change for the better.

Acceptance by the law-enforcement community was a rite of passage for the program, and for me. These were the people who understood the impact of what we were doing. But my job with the program made me the pariah of Russell's friends and my own family and friends, all of whom thought the program was about a bunch of bleeding hearts letting criminals out on the streets again. But I knew better. I was proud of the work I was doing.

After getting laid off I embarked on a search for another meaningful job, but wasn't having any luck.

"This is a perfect time to start a family!" my Mom glowed.

"Think about it! It's a real opportunity. It's not as if you're doing anything else," a chorus of cousins and friends observed.

True. I wasn't worth much in my current state, was I? It was a perfect time to bring new life into the world. I was born for this, wasn't I, to get married and have babies? Except it wasn't a perfect time for new life, at least not for me and Russell.

Our relationship was rocky even before we got married. There were so many differences between us! Even the minister who married us counseled against our getting married! But I was determined to do something right in my life, something my parents and whole family could finally approve of.

Before my engagement to Russell I felt like a tremendous disappointment to my family. Every guy I chose became someone my parents hated. But in fairness, they hated all my friends. Not that I had many girl-friends. I had one from college: Suzanna. After every fight Mom and I had, the accusations began.

"Did you run crying to her again?" she'd ask, sarcastic through a cigarette smoke screen.

"As a matter of fact, I did!" I'd say, falling into the trap.

"Did she hold your head in her lap?"

"I guess so."

"I'll bet she did. Did she kiss you and rock you too?"

I knew she was getting at something, but was too stupid to understand.

"She's my friend. At least someone cares about how I feel." I still didn't get it.

"I knew it! I knew you were lesbians!"

Wow, I went from being a street-walker going with any man who came my way to being a lesbian.

What chance did I have with the rest of the world if this is how my mother saw me?

I lost hope that anyone could see *me*.

But finally, there was light at the end of the tunnel. Nobody had to see me. All they had to see was Russell Knight.

My parents, especially Mom, loved Russell. That is, they loved his dark brown hair and gray eyes, lean athletic good looks, and Anglo background. Russell grew up in Newton, an upscale suburb of Boston known for its beautiful homes, close proximity to Boston proper, and excellent public schools. After graduating high school he wasn't really interested in the college scene. Instead he took off with a few buddies and began touring the East Coast with the idea of playing at each golf course. He didn't get very far, and ended up attending Nassau Community College on Long Island in New York, so he could combine getting a certificate in Business with being a beach bum. He didn't finish the certificate program, but since he found a good job in Manhattan, his academic career was not an issue. The important thing was Mom always wanted a non-Mediterranean-looking family, and with Russell she could finally have it.

There were other points in his favor apart from having a good job. He wasn't a long-haired musician or a rebel with a cigarette hanging out of his mouth riding up our driveway on a huge motorcycle like some of my former boyfriends. He didn't have a Latino or Pakistani last name. He wasn't Black. He had a posh Boston accent. I had managed to attract a bona fide White Anglo-Saxon

Protestant American with a normal haircut, and the family wasn't going to let him go.

After our wedding, I didn't tell anyone what life with Russell was like. The disconnect began during the wedding reception. After we walked around to all the tables of well-wishers thanking them for coming to our special day and collecting their envelopes and presents, Russell disappeared. I couldn't find him anywhere. The night was a whirlwind of emotion and music and hugging relatives. I didn't have much time to figure out where he was.

After the reception was over we drove back home to his apartment. I had my clothes with me but when I dragged my luggage into the bedroom I found out there was no place to put anything. Russell, the solicitous fiancée, hadn't made room in his chest of drawers or the closets for my things prior to my arrival. Not even a spare hanger. I felt confused and rejected.

His friends followed us home and while I sat in the bedroom trying to figure out where to put my stuff, he and his buddies sat at the dining table far into the night smoking cigarettes and pot, drinking Jagermeister, and counting all the money we'd been given as wedding presents. Knowing my generous family and friends I can believe it was a lot of money. Russell took it all and put it in one of his bank accounts I guess. He must have thrown out the cards we received so I never found out who gave what to us.

I never found out what happened to the Russell I thought I married either. The generous, considerate, good-natured boyfriend immediately became a controlling yet distant husband.

I walked around the apartment in shock those first few weeks trying to decide if I was still alive. Was there a pulse? Was there life after the death blow of the wedding?

I had thought a honeymoon would wean us away from Russell's friends and the routine of his pre-marriage life into a life more our own. He didn't want a honeymoon at all but he acquiesced to a week in Bermuda so he could golf at the world-famous Fairmont Southampton Golf Club with all the blue bloods. I don't golf – I tried to learn early in our relationship, but since I was only a beginner I ended up golfing alone because Russell didn't want to be held back from a serious game by playing with me.

I had already been to Bermuda several times with friends, but it is a beautiful island so I took what I could get. Russell golfed every day, and found a bunch of guys that were interchangeable with his usual cronies so he could hang out at the hotel bar every night.

I went alone to Horseshoe Bay or Jobson's Cove to enjoy the gorgeous pink sand and amazingly clear water, and do some snorkeling. We were on separate honeymoons.

When we got back, he picked up where he left off. I was still getting used to the idiosyncrasies of his apartment. Strange pale, flat bugs lived in the cupboards. Neighbors whose names I did not know nodded to me in benign greeting. The icebox part of the refrigerator wasn't working because it was full of holes Russell had made trying to chop away ice with a screwdriver. He insisted I should "just get another fridge from the building", but the Super regarded me with mistrust as I tried to explain where the holes in the icebox had come from. I'm pretty sure he thought I was responsible.

The neighbors were the best part of our apartment's cul-de-sac. There weren't a lot of them, and when I said hello to any of them they responded as if I was a normal person like they probably were. Maybe getting married was a good idea after all. I *was* maturing, understanding the real world instead of the buffered realm inside my head.

Russell and I parked our two cars on the narrow street, always finding spots right in front of our patio. Russell might be out with some friends or passed out after too many beers, but there I'd be on a nice fall Sunday afternoon dragging out two heavy buckets of water and two big sponges, one for soaping and one for rinsing, to wash the cars.

That's where I met Lara. My beautiful, funny friend. A friend for life.

CHAPTER SIXTEEN

I knelt next to my car with a soapy sponge in hand, right knee on the sidewalk and left hand holding the door handle of my car, hair hanging in my face, concentrating on soaking and scrubbing the accumulation of mud and road grease encrusting the bottom of the door and sides. I heard a car door slam and then a voice spooled out into the air like a colorful filament.

"You must be some kinda eejit! What were ya thinkin'?" A floating female voice.

"Come on Lara! It wasn't my fault! How was I supposed to know he was dead?" A male voice, holding back a laugh.

"Well if you ever listened to a thing *I* say, you'd know yer man was in the beyont now, wouldn't you!" The two voices laughed together.

I wanted to see the owners of these voices, his American, hers something else, but it seemed weird to stand up suddenly from behind my car as if I had been spying on them. What to do? While I deliberated, they reached the sidewalk.

"Ah, Danny, we have company," said the female voice.

I craned my head up to see unusually rich dark auburn hair sweeping against white skin and a perfectly straight nose as she turned her head to look at Danny, who stood beside her.

I dropped the sponge to the curb, pulled myself up, shook off the soap, and put out my damp right hand. "Hi. I'm Evie."

He was tall with dirty blonde hair, striking blue eyes, and a collegiate look. "I'm Dan." He took my hand firmly with an open smile.

"I'm Lara." The girl pointed her chin toward the building, a friendly smile overtaking her face. Her nose, cheeks and collarbone were dusted with light brown freckles. "We're over in 5A. Yer new around here," she added.

"Yes, I'm over in 5E," I said, pointing to our patio. "Just married. To Russell Knight."

"We know Russell," said Dan, in a way I interpreted as cautiously encouraging. "A fun-loving guy. You golf? I think I saw some clubs in his red Chevy."

"Yes, Russell is a dedicated golfer. It's nice to meet both of you. I hope I see you around." I poked at my sponge with the toe of my sneaker.

"Likely you will," said Lara. "Danny and I are just married too." She couldn't hold back a full-watt smile as she turned her face into his shoulder, and he pulled her to him with a grin.

I had to grin too; they were contagious. A thought of the strained existence with my own husband flashed quickly through my mind and I pushed it aside.

She looked toward me again and continued, "Danny usually works on weekends. If yer around one Saturday maybe we'll get lunch."

Shocked by an overture of friendship, I hesitated and then said, "Sure! I'd like that."

"Next week then. I'll stop by real quick durin' the week and we'll make a plan," she said, still smiling, then in a smooth motion she turned and started walking toward 5A.

"Nice meeting you," Dan called over his shoulder, catching up with her.

The two walked off hand in hand, swinging their arms back and forth. I went back to my muddy sponge, but now I felt good. I might actually make a friend. Did I even know how? The prospect was exciting and nerve-wracking.

My friendship with Suzanne hadn't survived very long after college. She was married soon after we graduated; I remained decidedly single. She quickly became a full-time mother; I worked full-time and was still living at home with my parents, seeing Russell, and spending alternate weekends in the Hamptons. Suzanne's main interest in me evolved into the possibility of me fulfilling the role of an 'aunt' who would baby sit for her young son. I wasn't interested. Whatever basis we originally had for our friendship died a natural death.

I missed the unique nurturing bond of a female friend. With Russell dictating all recreational activities I didn't have much time to make new friends. I don't think I knew how to be a real friend.

Now I had an opportunity to get to know a new person.

Lara and I hit it off and quickly became good friends. Our first lunch consisted mainly of Lara revealing every detail of her life in animated and hilarious fashion. She was twelve years younger than me, bursting with energy and enthusiasm, and with seventeen years of life under her belt and parental permission, she had recently married Dan. Her parents must have seen they were truly in love.

Lara was born on a sheep farm on the Dingle Peninsula in Ireland. She described the farm as a place of verdant green pasture, shifting mist, and stony inclines perfect for climbing and hiding. When the fog rolled back she could look down on the port of Dingle, with its roof tops and fishing boats clustered tightly together below the hills of the farm. Though it had less than 2,000 people, a trip into Dingle was always an exciting diversion from daily chores and the solitude of grass and stone.

Lara Gallagher came to the States as a ten-year-old when her family relocated from Dingle to the densely populated city of Yonkers on the outskirts of New York City. There her father found work as a building Superintendent and all-around handyman in the thriving community of Irish expatriots. Mrs. Gallagher woke up at 4 a.m. as she'd done on the farm and baked bread – real Irish whole grain bread – which she sold to local bakeries. Lara was the youngest of four children, born when her mother was 'past her prime' as Lara would say. Her two older brothers were quite a bit older than she was, and were almost like uncles to her. The brothers moved to other states once they were grown; she didn't see much of them. Her sister Belinda eventually moved back to Ireland, but she and Lara were close, always writing and calling even if they couldn't see each other very often.

In a way Lara was an only child. We bonded as if we were sisters.

When we were together it was hard for us not to laugh the whole time. Everything and everyone who crossed our path became funny. She was nearly eighteen years old now, her joy in life was palpable, and she wanted to start a family. She and Dan were trying hard to get pregnant. Each time she and I met, Lara would update me on their progress or lack thereof. As the weeks turned into months and there was still no child in the making, Lara kept up her positive attitude but I could tell it was beginning to wear on her.

"I know you want a baby, but you have so much time. I think you're putting too much pressure on yourself."

"I know, I know. But I want it *now*. Danny and me, we're *so* ready. Why is it that people who want a baby can never seem to have one."

"They do, all the time. You have to let it come naturally. No stress. Stress is a killer. It affects fertility, you know." The wise older woman offering sage advice to the inexperienced girl. Except the girl's life was on track, while the wise woman's was a disaster.

One chilly Saturday afternoon in February, Lara and I met in her apartment for tea. She fixed the best tea, Earl Grey with sugar and real cream. We spread Irish butter on warm slabs of her mother's delicious bread, sipped our tea, and she told me her news.

"We did it, Evie! Danny and me, we're goin' ta have a baby!" She was almost crying with relief, but pushed at her eyes with long fingers to keep the tears inside. I noticed for the millionth time her auburn hair was several shades darker than her tawny eyes, and I wondered what their baby would look like. Dan was a handsome guy, with his light hair and blue eyes. Their child was going to be gorgeous.

I felt a pure happiness for Lara. It felt clean. There was no competition between us. While I understood Lara's drive to start a family, I didn't want a child. Not at this point in my life. My relationship with Russell was enough work, and now was certainly not the right time for us to start a family. But my misfortune had nothing to do with Lara and Dan. She was deeply happy in her life and ready for more. I wanted this joy for her.

Hell, I wanted it for myself. But I couldn't have it.

It was a wonderful time for my young friends. She began to glow with the expectant mother aura. She saw her doctor regularly, took all the vitamins, and had all the tests. At around three months the first ultrasound was done, showing the small peanut growing within. We were all hushed when we looked at it together, Dan, Lara and I. There was something almost holy about watching the small being lie peacefully, protected, taking form at its own pace. They were excited and joyful, and I shared in their happiness in spite of myself. I never dreamed I could become a mother, but it was beautiful to watch someone who had. My friend was beyond happiness. She was transfixed with awe and love.

At around six months something went wrong. One day Lara started to bleed, and she felt sick to her stomach. She tried to be calm and insisted it was a normal stomach upset and everything was going to be fine. When the next day came and with it more dark blood, she first became hysterical, and then despondent. An emergency visit to the doctor confirmed a miscarriage but Lara already knew her baby was no longer alive.

She couldn't speak, couldn't respond, she went through the motions. Dan was filled with grief and anger, but what could be the focus of his anger? God or fate?

She was taken to the hospital in tears and came home a pale wraith of the woman she had been only a few days before. Her baby was gone for reasons unknown. Her heart was broken.

Dan had no idea how to console her, or himself. I didn't have many ideas either. Luckily her mother was there to care for her day and night. With her mother and Dan by her side, Lara was in good hands.

I ran errands for them or sat with her, holding her hand with not much to say. It seemed silence was best. I didn't know exactly what she was feeling, but I tried to feel it with her.

I think they used to call it a nervous breakdown. Whatever it's called, Lara had one. It destroyed her mentally and physically. She was eighteen years old when she and Dan went back to Ireland. Lara's sister Belinda ran a bed and breakfast in Fossa, a suburb of Killarney. A change of scene would be good for the young couple; she and Dan could help out at the bed and breakfast or try to find work around Killarney. There were some shops and restaurants, farms, households.

Saying goodbye was devastating to me. I knew we would stay in touch, but Lara hadn't even left yet and I already felt lost. What would my days be like if I couldn't look forward to laughing and having some tea together? I got Belinda's address, and felt like I was losing the best friend I had ever made in the world. I prayed Lara would be safe in Ireland. I prayed she and Dan would find peace in new surroundings that wouldn't remind them of this awful time.

I was a reminder of this time and place. It was only right that Lara should leave me here. We knew it wasn't forever.

CHAPTER SEVENTEEN

I was in my own sleepwalking horror movie. The weekends, which had been a time for me to connect with Lara and Dan throughout the fall and winter, were now devoted to me being on my own while Russell golfed with his friends, or driving to the condo late on alternate Friday nights so we could spend the weekend with his friends in the Hamptons.

Being endlessly cheap, Russell bought a little red Chevy Chevette that was more tin can than car. It usually wouldn't start if it was raining or humid, so depending on it for a weekend trip to the ocean was out of the question. My car was beaten into the ground while his stayed cute and shiny in front of the apartment, rather like the face Russell showed to the world.

We usually arrived at the beach condo around midnight. After unwinding and catching up on everyone's news, the wives, girlfriends and non-drunks tried to get some sleep. Getting any rest in the small condo was a challenge with the core group of guys laughing at each other's drunken antics, or cursing roundly when their card games became more heated as the night wore on.

Eventually there would be quiet. Russell usually passed out in front of a half-empty glass of beer, an un-played hand of cards and his hair fanned out across the wooden dining table like a melted mask.

I'd leave him there; he was too big to move and anyway he snored, so it was better to let him sleep where he was.

My presence wasn't necessary for him to continue with this life. My existence, friends, interests and dreams were pushed aside.

In front of the family he was funny and warm. At home he was distant and put me on a cash allowance. While I was still working, I was not 'allowed' to do anything with my paycheck other than deposit it into a joint savings account. Russell gave me $50 cash each week out of which I paid my weekly expenses, including public transportation from our apartment in Yonkers to Criminal Court in Lower Manhattan, and of course meals, drinks and all other weekend expenses. He had credit cards and as much cash as he wanted but he often borrowed cash from me, leaving me with even less.

There was no questioning the arrangement. Russell simply did not discuss things. If I brought up something I wanted to talk about, he would smirk and ignore me.

I was naïve. My parents had groomed me to be someone's wife by keeping me as sheltered as possible, but had not thought about teaching me how to pick a partner or understand what a partnership is. They were mainly focused on appearances and convention rather than the actual workings of the world. Only now does it dawn on me they couldn't teach me what they didn't know themselves.

I should have watched Russell's Mom and Dad at the dinner table if I wanted to know my future –

she silently serving the food, and he with his face turned down to his plate. Mr. Knight was an avid golfer and 'man's man', while she was a perfect 'homemaker'. The only conversation I heard between them was when Russell's father said something like, "Pass the peas." He didn't even use her name or say please.

That was how Russell learned how to be a husband.

We fought a lot about everything. I wasn't used to being on an allowance, especially when I was earning money I was not allowed to touch. My parents may have been old-fashioned and hovering but they were generous. Money had never been a sore point in our home.

He brought out the worst in me. I was reduced to pounding my fist on the table and yelling into Russell's face to get his attention when I wanted to talk about something, to no avail. He simply did not respond. I wasn't used to being totally ignored.

Or was I? Thinking back on the relationship, Russell and I always did exactly what he wanted. All our activities revolved around his friends and hobbies. Did this feel familiar because my interests and talents had been pushed aside as unsavory or dangerous by my parents as I was growing up?

At least I knew my original reasons for marrying him, even if they quickly evaporated. Or that's what I told myself. I asked him why he married me; he just smirked and said he liked the way I looked.

This was a time when the Women's Rights movement was starting to be real. I was all for it. I was tired of the Playboy centerfold hanging on the living room wall in the beach condo as a centerpiece for some of the guys to comment on the assets of the nude airbrushed image, and then compare it to all of us real women like we were ugly dogs. I was tired of being on an allowance. I didn't understand the expectation of my role as invisible waitress on monthly poker night, serving food and drinks to ten loud, table-pounding, cigar-smoking men while never being acknowledged, invited to play – I lived there too – or given an option of going somewhere else with my own friends. I was supposed to be available to serve the men like a shadow.

I had vowed to make the marriage work, but it wasn't working. Never having been a domesticated girl, I was not a waitress kind of woman.

After I lost my job my days were free. I cried all day long after Russell went to work and I was on my own left to contemplate my stupidity. I couldn't confide in my parents; they had to see how unhappy I was but never said anything. I couldn't burden Lara and Dan with my personal failure; they were across the ocean in Ireland healing their own hurts. I had made a mistake and I was going to have to live with it. I was convinced this was my penance for having been stupid and selfish all my life.

At the Hamptons condo, some of us would stay up late playing guitar and singing while the drunks played cards and eventually passed out. I made friends with Tommy, one of several young guys who were friends of friends. We talked about our dreams and our love of music. Everyone noticed my singing voice. "You should be a singer," they'd say, unaware of what it would take and of how impossible it seemed to me. I sang my heart out, laughed and joked with everyone, but Tommy saw through me.

"You don't look very happy," he said one night after everyone had either gone to sleep in their rooms or passed out in heaps at the tables or on the floor.

I was surprised he even noticed. Did everyone see how unhappy I was? It felt strange to confide in him but I needed to tell someone. "You're right. I'm not," I answered.

"I notice you and Russell don't have much in common."

"No, I guess we don't. Anymore."

"Well, you don't have to stay married, you know."

"Of course I do!"

"Just get a separation and see how it goes. Nothing final, it would be a trial."

"A separation?"

"Why should you be miserable?"

Good question. I think I let myself be miserable because after all the years of being restricted and told I had no talents and couldn't do anything valuable, I believed down to my soul my own happiness didn't matter. I had no self-image and no self-respect. I made a mistake in marrying Russell and hurt everyone else through my own stupidity. I truly believed I deserved to pay with my life.

No sooner were my blinders removed during a simple five-minute discussion with Tommy than I found out I was pregnant.

I was using birth control, an IUD which made me bleed all the time and often made me double over in pain. Russell wasn't concerned, as long as it would prevent us from having children. How bad could the pain be? I wasn't dead yet.

Russell and I didn't discuss birth control anyway; it was my job to take care of it. He wasn't ready to give up his image as a bachelor with no entanglements and no one to answer to. Most of the time he acted like he wasn't married.

I think the IUD failed because it may not have been placed correctly to begin with. Whatever the reason, now I was going to have a baby.

It was the *wrong* time. I had to get away from Russell, not start a family with him. I had to get a separation, or die of sorrow.

I fell into a depth of despair and confusion. What was I supposed to do now?

It was 1979. The Women's Rights movement had started when I was still in high school, and now that I was in my twenties it was bringing about some dramatic changes in people's everyday lives, and in some states' laws.

Women's Rights went against everything my mom had been trying to teach me all those years when she instructed me how to sit in a chair or told me I mustn't do all the things I dreamed I could do. No wonder I wanted to embrace it.

My best friend was far away in Ireland trying to pull her life together after having been devastated by a miscarriage. I was not going to share this problem with her. I was afraid to confide in my parents and ask their advice. There was no one to tell me what I should or could do. I was going to have Russell

Knight's baby. I had to discuss it with him. I had to make one last effort to do something right.

I remember the evening I told Russell. He came home late on a Friday night, three sheets to the wind. Maybe my timing was bad, but if I had waited until Saturday morning he'd already be on the golf course or we'd be at the Hamptons where he'd be breakfasting on beer and hard-boiled eggs so he could produce the world's most disgusting farts – his Saturday goal – so I don't think my timing mattered.

I tried to get his attention over dinner. He had a way of doing silly things that seemed cute to an outsider but were his way of blowing me off.

"Russell, we need to talk about something," I said simply, looking directly in his eyes.

"What, you silly Rabbit!" he said, and got up from the table with a cute grin at the same time that he bent over me and rubbed his knuckles into the top of my head as hard as he could.

"No Russell, really. This is important." I shook my head and tried to make eye contact again as he stood over me.

"What could *you* possibly have to say that's so impawtant, Rabbit?" Still grinning, but a little Boston coming out.

"I'm pregnant." I waited to see what he would say. I thought this should be big news.

"No, yawh not. You can't be. Yawh using that thing," he said with his broadest Boston accent. He abruptly walked out on me and into the living room, where he flopped onto the couch and switched on the TV to watch a sports program with the volume turned way up.

I got up from the table and followed him, raising my own volume to be heard. "Yes, the IUD that makes me bleed all the time. Something went wrong and now we're going to have a baby. We have to talk about it!"

"I don't have to talk about it. It's simple. I don't want it."

"What do you mean?"

"I mean. I. Don't. Want. It." He wasn't grinning anymore. I was no longer Rabbit.

"But it's *yours!*"

"How do I know whose it is? Yawh always playing guitar with that guy Tommy, and who knows what you do all day long." Wow. That was clear.

"It *is* yours. I'm not doing anything."

"I don't care what you do, but I don't want a kid. Anyway, you can get rid of it. It's not that big of a deal." He turned back to the TV and started playing around with the remote.

I was stunned. I had been planning to separate from Russell and the timing was terrible for us to be pregnant, but he didn't even want his own child. He was telling me to "get rid of it", to use his phrase.

What should I do? I couldn't tell my parents. They wouldn't even understand what I was saying if I told them *I'm going to have a baby,* and then, *by the way, I'm getting a separation from Russell.* Even if they'd have me, there was no way I could go back home to live with my parents while I was pregnant.

But if I separated from him, continued the pregnancy, and went out on my own, where would I go? How would I live?

There were only two things to do. Get a separation from Russell. And get an abortion.

CHAPTER EIGHTEEN

I know now as I never knew then we were all duped and confused by peer pressure, magazine articles, news media, movies, and each other. Women's Rights started out as a movement to enable women to become more educated, independant, and creative. It ended up being used to fuel the 'Sexual Revolution', in which so-called liberated women became the providers of free sex with no strings or stigma attached – for the men.

Women were liberated now, right? We were making our own decisions about our own bodies now, right? Some may have seen through the facade, but most women went from being a kind of guarded chattel carrying an untouchable treasure to being interchangeable nobodies providing sex in hopes of receiving love.

Perhaps some women *felt* liberated. Remaining chaste became an old-fashioned thing of the past. Valuing one's self was an outmoded notion. The denial of women's sex drive was at an end. As Mom always said, "You can't beat Nature". Many young women didn't know about contraception, or didn't know how to get a prescription for birth-control pills, or didn't even have a doctor. There was minimal sex education in the schools or in the home. What were the chances of getting pregnant anyway? So many guys said they were sterile from taking various drugs.

And if something happened, there was a choice now. Abortion became legal in the United States in 1972. Liberation ended up meaning murder. It wasn't simply the murder of a thought, a glimmer of life, a promise. It was the murder of self-respect.

It was the murder of a physically premature being whose soul was fully intact.

I didn't think that way then, but I think that way now.

Back then, I thought of a newly fertilized egg as a parasite, not yet human, and myself as an unwilling host. I was shocked at Russell's reaction, but his words began to sink in.

"It's not that big of a deal."

I confided in a few other people. Everyone said the same thing.

"It's not that big of a deal."

Did liberation mean I could decide for life or death according to *my* need?

Of course, from the dawn of time women had already been doing exactly that. Starting in ancient times, women employed methods such as binding or strenuous exercise to miscarry a fetus, or used certain plants as contraceptives or abortifacients. It was only in the early 1800s that abortion began to be criminalized. In modern times knowledge of natural contraception was lost, and naïve women became pregnant. Desperate women often put their lives in peril to terminate a pregnancy.

With the advent of legal abortion there was a much less dangerous choice, at least physically. I was already fully, actively living, if you could call it that. Was I more important because I had already been born? Was the wish of my husband important? Was our defunct relationship a factor?

I discussed my predicament with my doctor. She was sad as we discussed my options.

"I want to keep the baby. I can be a single mother," I said.

"How will you work? Do you have a support system?" she asked. "Women who succeed as single mothers have strong family support to help out with the baby, a home, and money."

"I don't know. I'm not sure how my parents will take the news." This was a lie. I was totally sure, and the idea of telling them I was going to have a baby *and* get separated was thoroughly terrifying.

"What about support? Does the father want to be part of the baby's life?"

"He doesn't want it."

Her face fell. "I know you want to keep this baby but I am recommending you give the idea a second thought. Being a single mother with no support or help from family is very difficult. You and your baby are in for a life on welfare. You're not going to be able to work for a long time after the baby is born. It's a very hard life. You'll be living in poverty, and you will be all alone."

Without a job and very little money, on the cusp of leaving my husband, I did not have to imagine how my parents would react if I showed up on their doorstep, literally barefoot and pregnant. All the accusations I'd lived with for years came flooding back.

"Trollop!"

"Street-walker!"

No, I wasn't going back to my parents.

I'm standing here in this place of light and sound and marvels and loved ones, and *I don't know.* I am fallible. I've done wrong and I've been selfish. I was weak and vulnerable. I felt totally alone. I was about to leave my husband. The father didn't want his child. My pregnancy was a subject I didn't have the courage to broach with Mom and Dad. I didn't give them a chance to show me a different side of them. I was sure they would castigate me for separating from or divorcing Russell, whom they adored, when I was about to have his baby. I couldn't count on anyone to help provide emotional or material support and care for me if I had a child as a single mother. And if I wanted to move beyond despair and keep on living, I had to get away from Russell. I was walking the edge of the abyss.

Bring the child into the world and then put it up for adoption? It was an option. I've known a few people who were abandoned by a parent or given up for adoption when their mother or family was in dire straits. They always seemed to be living in uncertainty, looking for a heritage, looking for the person who gave them away. It sounded like a terrible life sentence for a child. And I would still have to find a way to live while I brought the child to term.

I was like a wild animal with its leg caught in teeth of steel.

I knew what I had to do.

I got my own apartment in October 1979, in a borderline neighborhood in the Bronx. It was a dilapidated cold-water flat for practically no rent, perfect for a girl with no income and no prospects and no self-respect.

I chose abortion. I made an appointment and went alone to the clinic one afternoon. I think I was punishing myself.

It was terrifying and it was final.

If Lara had been there I know she would have come with me so I wouldn't have had to be alone, but she and Dan were still in Ireland recovering from the pain of their miscarriage. I never let her know I was pregnant; why should I burden her with even the thought of my problems? Should I have told her? Would she have convinced me to have the baby? Or adopted it? Or perhaps she would have encouraged me to go to my parents for help. I don't know. I didn't give her or my parents or myself or the baby the chance to find out.

I thought it was over but apparently, it's not.

Astara's child lived for a few minutes and then died despite her efforts to keep the child alive. Her heart was so broken she tried to kill herself but in the end, she chose life even though it meant pain every day. Shanara was her child and she loved her with all her heart and soul. Astara knew from the moment her pregnancy began that even though she had never planned to have a child, wasn't ready for it, and might even lose her place within her tribe, Shanara was a person with a soul.

Lara and Dan didn't have to question whether their unborn baby was a person with a soul.

My baby may not have seen the light of day, but now I know it was a person with a soul. It wasn't a parasite!

I made a *big* mistake. I thought I knew what it was to be liberated. I believed a fetus at eight weeks is not yet human. I was wrong.

That's what all this has been for. I need to find my child.

CHAPTER NINETEEN

I'm pretty terrified, walking around in circles on the grass. I know it's a girl but I don't know her name. Will she wait in the white place or will she come here to wait for another person, another likely fit for her very own original, beautiful soul? Is she within the edge of the forest? Is that why Lil Tux and Boozer stay near here?

I should be able to feel her. I know her. I'm sure I'll recognize her as soon as I see her. She has lain dormant, waiting for the right moment.

I walk around for an interminable time but she's nowhere to be found. She's not here, and I don't know how to find her.

There's a fuzzy shape ahead. It becomes more defined and familiar. The shape is walking, it has four legs, it's talking, and I know the voice.

"Hi, Mom."

"Hello dear. We've missed you so."

"Hi, Dad."

"Hello Evie. It's good to see you again."

I am about to say something snide out of habit, but catch myself. "It's good to see you again too. You look well." I never thought I'd see them again, yet here they are.

Dad *does* look well. His hair is thick and black with a few steely streaks, and he is obviously a lot stronger than the last time I spoke to him, which was right before the massive heart attack that took his life.

"I'm looking for someone. Do either of you know something I don't know?"

"I'm sure we do. It's funny to hear you ask, if you don't mind me saying so. We could never tell you anything." Dad raises his voice a bit but at least he's smiling.

"Don't start, Frank. How is the child, Evelyn?"

She means Lilly. "Fine. You can check on her anytime. Or are you having too much fun these days with your parents and brothers to take the time?"

"That's not nice, dear. You know I gave up my life to raise her."

"Not really. All you had to do was take care of Lilly like any other child. You had complete control over her life. I think she was the perfect child for you." I feel horrible and somewhat vindicated all at once. Why does nothing change? I had hoped that being here would at least change me.

"Well dear, at least I took on my responsibilities like a proper mother." Ouch. She must know who I'm looking for.

"Mom, I'm looking for a child." Might as well jump in with both feet.

"I'm glad you can finally see her, dear. I know we weren't much help to you. We always wanted to help, but we didn't always know how."

"It's not your fault. I would never have told you or Dad I was pregnant. I was too afraid of your reactions, but I should have trusted you."

"I understand dear, and I don't blame you. If I had known about Liliana when she was conceived I would have wanted an abortion myself."

I was shocked and suddenly very angry. "Don't ever say that! *Just don't!*"

"We all have our foibles. Do you want to know what happened to yours?"

Very arch. Mom hasn't lost her quick wit.

"Where can I find her?"

"You already did. She's Ashley!"

Ashley! I should have known! Maybe I did know all along.

Ashley is the newest love of my life, back when I had a life. She is Lara and Dan's daughter, turned two years old shortly before I began my out of body journey. Lara was fifty-three years old when she and Dan finally adopted. Which goes to show you there's always a chance for something wonderful to happen in life.

Lara's sister Belinda returned to Ireland in her early twenties, and ended up marrying and raising a family there. Belinda's daughter Jillian was born in 1975 and Belinda's granddaughter, Keira, was born in 1998. Keira became pregnant when she was only fourteen years old, and ended up having her child, Belinda's great-great granddaughter, in 2013. Ashley is that child.

Lara and Dan returned to the states a few years after their miscarriage. Their hearts had healed, and they still wanted children. But try as they might they were never able to conceive again. Lara learned to live with the fact that her dream of having a big family was not going to materialize.

She and I often talked about how she had always wanted children of her own, and how different hers and Dan's life would be if they could have raised a family with lots of kids.

By the time Ashley was born, Mr. Gallagher had passed on and Mrs. Gallagher was a spry ninety-five years old – too old to fly – but Lara and Dan went to Ireland to see Belinda and all the children and children's children. With the support of her family young Keira had taken her pregnancy to term, but she was still a child herself.

Lara was fifty-three years old. This wasn't her own child, but it was so close. Opportunities were running out. What would Dan think? It turns out the baby was a blessing for both of them.

Lara and Dan adopted Keira's baby girl in Ireland, and came back to the states with her. They named her Ashley.

It's an incredible story. It showed me what family can do for each other. Where there is trust there is no shame or recrimination. Keira gave up her baby knowing the child would always be part of her family.

I remember thinking at the time – a fleeting thought – what if I had told my parents? What would have happened?

Too late for me and my child. I focused on Lara and Dan's daughter Ashley, and the family they were finally going to have. I felt profoundly happy for my friend. She was going to be a wonderful mother.

Inexplicably, I loved that little girl from the very first time I saw her. She wasn't a newborn anymore, she was nine months old. I couldn't get over her face so filled with unique character and intelligence! The white skin, curls of dark red hair on a perfectly round head, and dimples everywhere. She looked so much like Lara!

I loved Ashley without understanding why. What was the connection? I thought it was the charm of her personality, or the red hair, or how her eyes turned very clearly hazel by the time she was a year old. Eyes like mine.

Is she the original soul of Shanara? Did Shanara try to come back into the world years ago, only to have *me* reject her? Has the soul of a lost child finally found its way to Ashley?

Is this knowledge a gift or a consolation prize? I'll never be able to talk to Ashley again or color with her or make her laugh. But at least my girl can have a life, the life I wouldn't give to her.

And don't forget, I remind myself, *she's not my girl anymore. I gave up that right.*

Wonders and mysteries abound. I'm speechless.

"You can still go there and say Hi. She'll have an Elmo backpack. At this age it's not frightening for them."

Mom and Dad are gone. When did they go?

I look around but there's nobody here. I could swear someone just told me to go one more time through that sticky soft separation and tell Ashley how much I love her.

CHAPTER TWENTY

I'm trying to get ready for this. If I look the way I did when I was younger Ashley may not even recognize me. That's probably the least of my problems. I push through the tackiness of air and cloud and light, looking for a little girl wearing an Elmo backpack.

A special girl. Her hair is a coppery auburn starting to curl at the ends, and her face is filled with joy, emotion, personality and intelligence. She has hazel eyes and a mouth like a rosebud. Dimples crop up all over her face depending on her mood.

Ashley laughs easily and speaks in the short, direct sentences of a two-year-old child. Every moment is a learning experience for her, and like all small children she takes in everything and spits it back at you with her own style. Her personality is already distinct. Ashley is a happy, creative child who doesn't hold back her emotions.

She started pre-school right after her 2nd birthday. The day Lara mentioned it to me I cried without knowing why. So young! Too young to ship her off to strangers. Who will change her diaper there? Who will understand how fragile her feelings are? Will she be fully indoctrinated by age three? Is there no room for individuality?

But I kept my mouth shut as Lara explained all the advantages of the pre-school, and I felt better hearing all the preparation with the mothers and their children before sessions started. It was only a half-day, a few hours. The school was right near home. There was nothing to be worried about.

Off to school she went. It was heart-rending for Lara and Dan, no matter how prepared they thought they were. Lara recounted with trembling chin how Ashley cried hysterically that first day, nonstop, for about an hour. She knew because she was parked right outside the school, listening to her child screaming for Mommy.

Finally, the crying stopped. When the two hours of school were up Mommy and Daddy were there to take her home again, and Ashley felt much better. As the days passed she had so much fun drawing pictures and learning new things, and it seemed that pre-school was good for her. Ashley was making friends and enjoying her young life. It was going to be okay.

I missed out on an important life experience. I was never a parent. I admit I don't know what's best for a child. The only child I ever knew was Lilly, and Ashley is nothing like Lilly. Lilly is soft and quietly mischievous and her future always had limitations. Ashley has a strong mind and a special bright spark. She has a flair for the artistic and musical, and is going to do exceptional things in her life.

Pushing now through the crystalline atmosphere I see there are many children outside the school. The teachers have them all in a line on the sidewalk, waiting for their parents to pick them up and bring them back to their homes.

It's a beautiful day on Earth. I think I hear her and look for Elmo, but a lot of the kids have Elmo backpacks.

Wait, I think I see her. There she is! But I can't talk to her now, not with all the other kids and teachers around.

The teachers are standing along the sidewalk watching the children like hawks, but keeping a little apart to let them feel somewhat independent. I float down feather light, lying in the arms of the wind blowing over Ashley's head, and watch her for a while. She is singing a song to herself, waiting for Mommy to pick her up.

"Hmm, hmm, star, star, twinkle high and high, Eh-sa and Eh-mo flying high and high, hmm, hmm..."

I float down until I'm right over her head. Her hair smells sweet and I see it appears to have been combed in places with something pink and sticky. Lara will have a fit! Ashley has covered the backs of her hands with heart stickers. Her finger tips are pink and purple. She loves to play with ink stamps.

"Ashley," I whisper in her ear, "it's Aunt Evie!"

She stops her song and cocks her head to one side, then smiles. "Evie, Evie," she whispers back. I know what she's thinking: where have I been? Has Paul come to visit without me?

"Hi Ashley, I've come to see you because I had to go away, but I miss you very much."

"Kay. You come now to play again?"

"I can't stay long. But I would like to hear about school."

"Pack!" She laughs and swings her backpack vigorously from side to side by putting her weight on one foot and then the other, her chubby legs spread apart and the knees slightly bent for good leverage. She makes a dance out of the motion. The pack is big for her small frame but she carries it well.

"Do you bring your lunch to school in there?" I ask her. She is so grown up.

"No. Books. And Eh-mo and Eh-sa."

"But no lunch?"

"Ordige and cheeth." Orange and cheese. I remember this Ashley snack.

"Do you like school?"

The face changes from a smile to a thoughtful look for a moment, then back to a smile. "Yeth! New friends. I like pack!"

"I'm glad you're having fun at school. Who is your best friend?"

"Jordan and Sammy. I love Sammy. I give him hugs!"

"I give Ashley a big hug too!"

"No Ashley kith?"

"Of course! The biggest kiss in the world is from me to Ashley."

I don't know how to do this. Will she feel something and get scared? Can she see me? I don't think so.

"I'm going to try to kiss you on the head," but she's already pointing her face upward with her mouth in a kiss pose. She must feel where I am though she can't see me.

I float down lower and try kissing her quickly on the cheek. I don't feel a thing, there's no sense of touch. It's probably for the best.

She waits in her pose. "Smack," I say, and make a loud kissing noise.

She opens her eyes and giggles with delight. "That not a real kith!" she says in her scariest monster voice.

"It's a good one though, isn't it?" I can't talk much longer. It's getting hard to do this.

"Good!" She's jumping with the excitement of being alive on a beautiful day. "Smack! Smack!" she shouts with each jump.

A dark red Land Rover pulls up to the curb, stops, and Lara opens the door and gets out of the car. She takes a few steps and kneels, smiling, with arms out wide.

"Ashley!"

"Mamma, Mamma" Ashley shouts, and runs joyfully to her mother.

Lara swings her up into the air and turns toward the back seat of the car with Ashley in her arms.

"Evie!" Ashley twists quickly back and forth in Lara's arms pointing and laughing at the air, the sky, the trees and the playground.

"Evie," Lara repeats slowly. The smile drops quickly. "Remember, she had to go away. She won't be visitin' us right now." She still has the same freckles I always loved. There are a few white hairs among the thick auburn now.

"No!" Ashley stares intently at where we had been talking a moment before.

Lara looks, but there's nothing there. Nothing.

Just me, invisible and insubstantial as ever.

They drive away but I remain. It's a perfect day but I can't feel the sunlight bathing every living thing on the planet. I don't want to leave again now that I know who Ashley is.

How can I leave? All my life I've spent without knowing what's next. I've been an aimless traveler without purpose. Am I done now? Is that it?

❧❦

I drift slowly away. I can't stay there any longer, the pain and confusion are overwhelming. I need to think seriously about what to do next.

As if I have a choice. I'm dead, or I'm in a coma. Is that what all the beeping noises are? Lately they have intruded into my drifting existence, a constant backdrop reminding me of everything I've thrown away so easily. Why is it beeping? Who is trying to save me?

"This is not all bad Evie. Think about how far you've come." A new voice, not a voice at all, but rather like a triad of tones drifting through me as if I'm a transparent thought. I'm back here where I belong in the white place of nothing, and this voice is talking to me as if it knows me. Do I know it?

"Who are you? Where are you? I want to see you before I say another word. No more games." That's me and I sound pissed! Is this what self-esteem sounds like? But I already know what it's like. Astara had so much self-esteem, all that Evie lacked.

I decide that I am simply not talking to anything invisible, and turn in a circle until I see it floating strangely near, elongated like a mermaid or an unfolding fetus with long, black hair that sweeps back and forth as if surrounded by a breeze or flowing water. It has a strange non-face and dark slanted eye smudges that pierce into a place I didn't know about before. It's not scary, but it's not human.

"You have a very interesting voice," I tell it. The entity inclines slightly toward me.

"I am happy you can finally see me. Most do not. I am all the missing parts of you. Some have called me the Oversoul. Others know that every soul starts out whole, but a piece breaks away to nurse each mortal wound. The soul is always in peril. Some wounds could destroy it forever. The wounds may have been dealt eons ago but never healed. Some are too heavy to carry along with the strife of living, so wounded fragments stay detached and waiting."

"What are you waiting for? You took your time to show yourself." I'm not even trying to hide my irritation. How many tricks are these beings going to play on me? Where is it going to send me now?

"You are at a crossroads, Evie. I will help you find your way home, wherever you want that to be."

"You're going to help me? If you're a piece of my soul why don't I know about you?"

"You are not meant to know everything. But I have come to help you choose your next stage. Live or die. It's all up to you. You are a being of Light.

You can always go back to the Light and start anew."

A being of Light. That sounds nice. The musical voice is seductive like a wind chime or birds trilling on an early spring day. It says I have a choice, and I believe it.

"I want to stop hating myself. I think that's what keeps me from doing the right things. Is there a chance to go back without anger or shame? I miss everyone back there. I miss Evie. If I could be myself I *know* I could finally do some good. Paul and I could enjoy life together again and not worry so much about who's right and who's wrong. I could keep doing everything for Lilly so she never has to be alone. And Ashley, I could see her grow up. I could be something to her. Could I do that?"

"Evie, you learned so much about life and loving when you lived as Astara. You can continue to learn even more as Evie if you allow it. Do you know why you stop yourself?"

"No. I wish I did."

"No matter. These are things you will learn for yourself. Or you may come to realize these obstacles are no longer important. Move forward Evie."

"What's the alternative?"

"You can always try again. There's a lot of time."

"Try *again*? I don't want to come back remembering nothing, and go through all the pain of growing up, not understanding my parents, and being awkward and confused! I want to come back to my now! I just found Ashley! I have Lilly to take care of. I have a life *now*, as Evie!"

It's sudden. I take in a huge hurting breath. It feels like I'm dying. Like I'm suffocating. Like I'm Astara under water, taking the deep breath she was afraid to take.

But I know this is not dying. This is living, and it hurts more than anything else has ever hurt me.

It's loud in my ears. It's my voice gasping for the real air of my real life.

My decision is made without knowing how I did it. It's time to breathe deeply and plunge in. I'm getting one more chance to live life as Evie.

CHAPTER TWENTY-ONE

I try to scream, thrash, or do anything. I can't move. I'm literally tied down.

I try to scream again but there's something down my throat. A tube! I'm choking!

No, something is breathing for me.

I hear beeps and a focal point of light glows above. What happened to the beautiful day? Where the hell am I now? I keep trying to set myself free of tubes so I can scream.

A face. Someone finally notices. The beeps must have changed. The dead do sometimes wake up.

Soon there are two faces leaning over me, not looking at me but at something behind me. Maybe the thing that beeps. They are wearing blue coverings over their mouths. I must be in a hospital. This is the last place I want to be. You can catch a lot of diseases in the hospital. HIV from blood transfusions, MRSA superbug infections from people who don't wash their hands.

Or is it the only place I want to be? I'm not clear about anything, but it appears I'm alive now and a minute ago, I wasn't.

A minute ago my arm was light and strong but now it weighs a ton. Everything hurts. I remember now. This is what it feels like to be alive.

Get these bindings off me! What are these people looking at? Can they see me? Does sound carry here? What happened to me? Does anyone besides these blue faces know I'm here?

They're going to ask me questions soon. What's my name? Evie. Evelyn. Where do I live? 310 Eagle Claw Road. Where was I? Someplace else where there were lots of souls I know, and a few I didn't. What do I remember before that? Falling down and not being able to move.

Have I been in a coma? Am I old now, eighty or ninety? By now everyone who knew me when I fell down is dead.

There is a commotion outside and then a man's face floats into place over my head. A doctor? A lawyer? He doesn't look like a religious figure, so at least this isn't Last Rites.

"Hi," says the face.

It's hard speaking around the tube.

"Soon," he says calmly, then calls loudly over his shoulder, "Nurse! We need someone in here!" His face comes back into view. He's smiling. Sure, why not, everything's going well for him.

I hear the door open and feel the air move as someone walks swiftly into the room. "Nurse, please remove these tubes. Miss D'Arico is awake."

Quickly the nurse leans over me and starts pulling something out of my throat. I had become used to the feeling and now that it's being removed the sensation is horrific.

Oh. God. My brain registers red but screaming is not an option. Even speaking is out of the question.

I'm breathing on my own now, making a soft noise with each breath to soothe myself. With a cold hiss, oxygen tubes are inserted into my nostrils. The beep continues in an unsteady rhythm. Is that my heart beat?

"Paul," I barely croak.

"Hold on. Be with you in a minute," says the doctor. He's looking at the beeping thing behind me and writing on a clipboard.

I don't care what the doctor wants me to do. I speak slowly and almost without sound. "Did. You. Call. Paul?" My throat feels like it's ripping apart. I've got to get out of here.

"Yes."

"Sure?"

"He's on his way. You need to rest. Stop trying to talk."

I fall into a time without thought or being. It feels like the next moment when I open my eyes to find the same doctor standing at the foot of the bed, his head bent over the clipboard. Is that all he does, play around with that thing?

His eyes shift to mine quickly. "Welcome back. Feeling better?"

I nod, experimenting with a swallow to see how much it hurts.

"I don't want you to speak but I need to check. Can you tell me your name, very softly?"

"I. Already. Told..." Oh, that was in my mind. I'm going to have to get used to how it works here all over again.

"Shh. Softly, remember?"

I whisper, "Evelyn. D'Arico. Call Paul. Now."

"All right, relax young lady. No more speaking for a while. Paul is on his way."

Young lady? I feel young and old and wise and stupid all at the same time. In other words, I feel like it's just another day.

❧

It's a beautiful day in early July, not too warm, not too humid now that the afternoon has burned itself out. Sitting outside on a lawn chair, I'm happy to simply feel sun on my arms and stare without thoughts into the small woods beyond the perimeter of my garden.

I recall the intense heat of afternoons by the Cliff, but that was then. The flute-like song of a Hermit Thrush moves right, left, up and back, but I can't spot him in the woods.

My garden is overgrown. I don't have the strength yet to do any real work and the weeds are lush and thriving. Paul planted some things for me to keep up appearances, but I have let go of worrying about how the garden looks. I will do better next year.

Yesterday marked my two-month waking-up anniversary. I collapsed in January and they tell me I was in a coma until I woke up in early May.

Nobody knew if I would ever wake up again except for Paul. He says that when he came to visit me each day he could see my eyeballs moving under my eyelids, so he knew I was on my way back. As Olive said, Paul was sure I would be coming home any day. He was right, and everyone else was wrong.

They say I had a stroke. Although I lost consciousness for months there doesn't seem to be any permanent damage to my brain. It's a miracle.

I've been doing traditional physical therapy for the past few weeks, and started doing Feldenkrais movement this week. I like Feldenkrais better than the traditional PT, so this Friday will be my last therapy session. I have another chance at life and this time I'm going to do what feels right.

The hardest thing has been to speak again. The tubes tore my throat and voice box, and for around two weeks I could barely whisper. Now that I can speak I have so much to say, but I don't know how to say any of it.

Eating has been difficult not only because of my sore throat but because I don't feel hungry. I don't even know what I like anymore, except for fish and herbal teas and a craving for fresh figs. The last time I ate I was Astara.

What a great homecoming! It was Paul and me and the cats. He decorated the house with a *Welcome Home Evie* banner and had stocked up on my favorite dark chocolate with almonds, which I was unable to eat for several weeks. Olive and Chloe were literally bouncing off the walls when I walked through the door. They didn't need any time to get used to Mommy being back. Moose flopped onto his usual spot on the couch, purring loudly, rolling around, and rubbing his nose on my hands and face. Paul said Moose didn't go on the couch at all during the months I was gone, but instead lay under my chair sighing all day. I miss being able to hear Olive's voice in my head, but I understand my animals as well as I ever did.

Paul has been so helpful around the house, vacuuming, shopping, and helping to make meals. My strength is returning bit by bit. I can barely do the walk into town and back. I still don't drive long distances. I'm in no rush.

Being indoors is strange. The ceilings seem low and the plaster walls are not alive. Time spent lying in the forest or in a painted cave by the sea listening to the ocean and the wind must have opened a lost part of my brain. I asked Paul if we can go camping sometime, but he's not an outdoor kind of guy.

I was so excited to see Lilly! We waited until I was moving around better so she wouldn't be alarmed. She was so happy to see me; we hugged and couldn't let go. I missed her so much, but the moment I felt her arms around me and looked down at her sweet face I was instantly restored. I will never leave her again. We don't talk about the day I came to see her. There's no need.

Lara started visiting me in the hospital right after I woke up. On her first visit she came into the room slowly, her tawny brown eyes looking wild. I think she wasn't sure if I would still be me after lying in coma for so many months. I assured her it truly *was* me through a series of hoarse whispers, smiles, and pantomimes, and she finally relaxed.

We hugged for long minutes, without words or tears. It was good to feel her warm hair next to my cheek. Good to feel myself back in the flesh, and not paying an invisible, unfelt visit from another place.

Once I came home Lara visited me at our apartment often; one day she'd bring her special Earl Gray tea, another day she'd bring her Mom's whole grain bread. Yes, her Mom is still baking bread!

Last week Paul and I visited Lara, Dan and Ashley at their house for the first time since I woke up.

I wondered how it would be. But Ashley didn't forget me. She remembers the day I came down to Earth to visit her. I haven't mentioned my visits to anyone and it's easy to cover up what Ashley is saying, but Lara looked at me strangely when Ashley talked about me giving her a big smack kiss from the sky.

How can I tell Lara what happened to me? How can I tell her who Ashley is? I don't think she needs to know.

I tell myself the important thing is that *I* know who she is. I'm thrilled to have the chance to see who she becomes. It's all I have, and I have made peace with it.

I miss seeing Uncle Larsson, but I talk to him and Aunt Toni every day. I miss my parents, truth be told, even though our meeting was not as productive as I would have liked. That was mostly my fault. I've started a journal where I write down conversations with Mom and Dad. Now that I know they are here with me I can work on our relationship. I remind myself how much they care, and that they are helping me as much as they are able from a place I can't see.

Knowing that Lil Tux and Boozer are safe and truly happy was worth the trip. So many nights before the coma I lay awake worrying about what kind of life my Boozer had, or crying over my Lil Tux's death. Now I know they are both safe. Now when I see Tux's shadow running beside me in the apartment I feel joy and I greet her because I know she hears me. It's a great relief to be heard.

I'm filled with awe and gratitude for the memories I have been allowed to keep but it's hard not being able to talk about everything that happened, or who I saw, or who I used to be. I thought I would want to tell everyone – I *do* want to tell everyone – but it's safer to keep my memories for myself to sift through and relive. Each time I remember what it was like to be Astara I am amazed and proud of myself. That was really me! My first life! I was amazing. That must mean I can be amazing again.

I've told Paul some things, but I don't know how to talk to him about Astara. Every day I think about how extraordinary she was. What damage must have happened to my soul since then, to deteriorate to the point I'm at now. Evie has always been such a weak, self-centered woman. I feel like I went backward in my evolution instead of forward.

Or maybe not. I've been reading a lot of books lately about near-death experiences and past life regression. There's a lot out there although nothing too clear. It's not as if you can prove any of it. I started reading Ralph Waldo Emerson's essay

"Nature" which talks about the early transcendental concept of the Oversoul. Is that who I met in the white place? It said it was a part of my own soul that had split off from the rest because it sustained mortal wounds. That entity was not a figment of my imagination; it was *real.* I'm glad it didn't tell me what the mortal wounds are. I don't think I can handle it.

I meditate each morning hoping to see some shred of what I experienced, but I never see anything. Sometimes I question myself: did it really happen? When there is nothing to hold onto but a memory it's hard to keep believing. I don't want the memory to fade, but each day I lose some of my experience outside of time and space, and return more and more to the third dimension of this physical world.

I've started writing a book so I can tell my story and not lose any more of it, although I don't think I will use my real name. I don't want the people who know me to think I'm crazy. Not even Paul will believe what happened to me, although I told him about how I hovered over the apartment and saw them taking me away. Because he was there too he remembers and believes me. But if I start explaining about how I woke up as a leaf, and then as Astara, well, I'm not going to tell anyone about that.

There's so much I have yet to learn. My goal for each day is to learn one more thing, to take one more step along my path. I don't know where the path leads but I know that this life I chose is the best way for me to get where I'm going.

There are so many souls traveling the same path, never seeing each other, yet walking side by side.

So many souls returning to the place where it all started, returning with our lessons intact even if not remembered.

So many souls, returning.

Returning.

ACKNOWLEDGEMENTS

Early in life I began writing poetry. I loved putting together a few words that stood out in a design against the white paper. Anything longer felt like I had been tossed overboard. I would surely drown there.

I certainly never thought I'd write a novel. Then one day about a year ago, I caught the last five minutes of a radio program in which a man named Tom Bird said anyone could write the bones of a book over four days' time.

I felt instantly excited. Skeptical. I knew it couldn't be done. I had to try. Actually, my first thought was I had to prove him wrong.

So began my journey back to myself. It is my journey of a lifetime. And I have many people to thank for helping me along my path.

I am grateful to Tom Bird, Sabrina Fritts, Mary Stevenson, and John Hodgkinson for giving me the focus, support and tools I needed to clear away the debris of self-denial and free up space for my novel.

I give thanks every day to the fellow authors who have been my daily confidants and friends: Debra Moody, Evelyn Foreman, Tim McKeever, Liz Onyeabor, Pamela Jean Horter-Moore, Susan MacIver.

I am grateful every day for Sharon CassanoLochman and Suzanne Singer: faithful friends, powerful women, and talented authors who continue to inspire me as fellow writers and beacons of light.

Thanks to the other readers of my impossible dream stories: Judy Colombo, Claudius Colombo, Mary Cavazis, Janice Biondo Zaring, Shiela McGayhey, and Michael Pasciolla. Your encouragement and enthusiasm for my writing journey gave me courage, especially in the early days when the characters in my novel were being born.

I extend my heartfelt thanks to the intrepid readers of my manuscript. Michael Pasciolla, thanks for being my partner and encouraging creative presence. Mary Cavazis, your critical reading and thinking improved so many parts of my book and kept my feet on the ground. Sharon CassanoLochman, your encouragement on the journey kept me positive and open when writer's block threatened to stall me. Georgina Kemm, your kindness and knowledge of shamanism and spiritual practices gave me confidence in the integrity of my story.

Though they probably do not realize it, the young mothers and beautiful children who grace my life are a constant inspiration to me. Seeing a mother's love for her child is essential for me to continue to have faith in the human race. Being able to play with small children has allowed me to tap once again into my own memories of childhood. I'm glad to say I have not really changed since I was three. Knowing the world through the eyes of a child confirms my suspicions that there is beauty and magic everywhere.

My gratitude goes out to each of my editors for your singular and essential insights, guidance, and lessons in voice, tense, and punctuation. I would not have completed this novel without your knowledge, experience and positive critiques: Idony, Ross Angelella, and Bill Worth.

My special and ongoing thanks goes to Denise Cassino: book publicist extraordinaire, guide and guardian of a neophyte author's sanity through the social media maze and the new rules of the publishing world, knower of all sources for book cover creation, web site development, and manuscript endorsement. Like a magician, you turn bits and pieces of nearly nothing into a polished finished product.

It was a wonderful experience working on my book cover with Debbie O'Byrne of JetLaunch.net. I did inundate you with emails, pins, and descriptions of what I thought I wanted. But as with so many things, what I wanted was right in front of me all the time. Thank you for seeing it, presenting it to me, and incorporating all my suggestions and desires to make a beautiful book cover for *Returning Souls*.

Thank you Ross Angelella, Sharon CassanoLochman, Georgina Kemm, and Bill Worth for your generous book endorsements.

Many thanks to the women of my Monday morning healing group. The journeys we took together woke me to my wind horse guardian and to the vision of the young girl who became Astara.

Thank you Michael Pasciolla for being my partner in this unexpected life. Thank you for always being on my side and believing in me, for reading my manuscript so many times, and for your honesty. Thank you for creating a logo to match my Wind

Horse vision, and for drawing your vision of the essence of my novel for the book cover. Thank you for your steadfast love.

Of the greatest importance are all the animals who have shared my life, including Tootsie and Alexander who were not my dogs at all but should have been. Brandy, I wish we had had more time together. Unending love and admiration goes to my courageous little friend, Squeaky. Raisin, you haunt me still. Gus, LuLu and Nikko, I love you three cats very much and will always do everything I can to keep you happy and safe, even though you wake me up at two in the morning just because you can.

Through it all, my parents and entire family are the bedrock upon which I have stood all these years. Woven into memories, adolescent angst, and the chasm between our generations, you are ever with me. Mom and Dad, I wish you could see that I've written a novel. I believe you do see it, and I hope you feel proud. Thanks for teaching me all that is right and good.

I owe everything I am and every valuable thing I know to my sister, Teresa. I am grateful she is here so we can continue on our own special journey together.

ABOUT THE AUTHOR

 Ernestine B. Colombo fell in love with words when she was a child. Writing became her daily ritual and passion. She earned a B.A. in Journalism from the The City College of New York, then finally landed a position at a huge banking corporation. The job became her life. The ritual of writing was forgotten.

Colombo retired in 2011. At first, she lost herself in the healing touch of her garden. Color and pattern took the place of fluorescent lights and deadlines. Seasons passed, the garden expanded, but there were no new words.

In 2016, she began a journey of the mind and heart. The result is her first novel, *Returning Souls,* the story of a woman who gets a second chance at life. Hopefully you will recognize yourself somewhere in these pages. You may even start believing we all get a second chance.

Colombo is winner of First Honorable Mention in the December 2017 Institute of Children's Literature PawSome Poetry Contest.

Ernestine lives in a suburb of New York City with her partner Michael and their three cats. She spends her time writing, working in her garden, and watching the hummingbirds go from flower to flower, taking a sip from each one.